HIGHWAY JUSTICE

The dirtbag reached inside the crashed BMW, grabbed an attache case, and ran hard toward the Leeco rig.

"Stop!" Marc yelled.

The man answered with gunfire.

Marc and Carl opened fire, Uzis singing a death chant that stopped the shooter in his tracks. He hung there, suspended by some unknown force, twitching rhythmically, for a long moment. He fired one last time as another volley of 9mm justice tore through him.

Finally the pistol lay silent beside the evil hand that held it. The man's other hand was wrapped around the handle of the attache case in a grip that even death couldn't separate.

The two warriors were already up and running toward the fallen man.

Bantam Books by Bob Ham:

Overload #1: PERSONAL WAR
Overload #2: THE WRATH
Overload #3: HIGHWAY WARRIORS
Overload #4: TENNESSEE TERROR
Overload #5: ATLANTA BURN
Overload #6: NEBRASKA NIGHTMARE
Overload #7: ROLLING VENGEANCE
Overload #8: OZARK PAYBACK

OVERLOAD, Book 8

OZARK
PAYBACK

Bob Ham

BANTAM BOOKS
NEW YORK · TORONTO · LONDON · SYDNEY · AUCKLAND

OZARK PAYBACK

A Bantam Book / December 1990

ISBN 0-553-28808-3

Published simultaneously in the United States and Canada

Bantam Books are published by Bantam Books, a division of Bantam
Doubleday Dell Publishing Group, Inc. Its trademark, consisting of
the words "Bantam Books" and the portrayal of a rooster, is
Registered in U.S. Patent and Trademark Office and in other
countries. Marca Registrada. Bantam Books, 666 Fifth Avenue, New
York, New York 10103.

PRINTED IN THE UNITED STATES OF AMERICA

RAD   0 9 8 7 6 5 4 3 2 1

This one's for Leslie—the most ideal daughter a man could have—whose creative mind thought of the original, basic idea.

May the sun always shine as brightly in your world as you have shined in mine.

Tootles

(Now, go clean up your room)

The trouble with the future is that it usually arrives before we're ready for it.

—Arnold H. Glasow

———

With drug abuse, there is no future. Each day is a new death over and over. The scourge is rampant on our nation and I will scour the land with cleansing fire until the villainous evil cowers for mercy.

—Carl Browne

OZARK
PAYBACK

Chapter One

1988

Larry Cummings awakened the very instant the Baby Ben alarm clock rang. He reached over to the small stand inside the Freightliner sleeper and shut off the clanging bell. His arms flew out and downward as he stretched them and his legs. Then he rolled over in the bunk and peeked outside. [It was raining hard. The third storm in less than six hours.]

Cummings thought about getting something to eat at the truck-stop restaurant across the lot, but one glance at his watch and he decided against it. He was already ten hours behind schedule. But come hell or high water, he was determined to get the load to the consignee on time. And that meant breaking the speed limit, but that's what the bird dog was for. When the little Escort radar detector chirped, it was foot off the pedal and easy down on the brakes. A few changes in the log book would satisfy even the most discriminating Interstate Commerce Commission inspector. No big deal, really, because everybody did it when they got a little off the beaten path of the assigned destination . . . at least everybody *he* hung around with.

When he threw off the blanket, Cummings saw the little brown vial he always kept under the mattress. He had forgotten to tuck it away when he finished with it last night. He picked it up and popped the plastic top. His index finger dipped inside and came out covered with off-white powder. He touched it to his tongue and

1

thought about taking a snort, but decided against it. He remembered that the reason he was already late was the cute little browned-haired truck-stop mama from last night and the fantastic white powder that had brought them together and kept them that way most of the night. Although she was just a memory from another one-night stand, at least the coke was still in the sleeper with him, and one out of two wasn't bad.

Cummings worked his way out of the sleeper and into the driver's seat. The Freightliner's idle sounded like a sleeping kitten's purr. Cummings looked at the fuel gauge . . . half-full. There was a thermos that should be full of coffee somewhere in the cab. Cummings looked for it under the clothes that cluttered the passenger's seat. He found it underneath his wrinkled jeans, but somehow during the night's activities it had slipped open and spilled. Cummings turned it bottom-side up and drained the last quarter-cup of cold coffee into the lid. Then he found his shirt, wrinkled like his pants, and rummaged through the breast pocket. They were there, pickle park specials: amphetamines.

His fingers were still asleep, lacking the agility necessary to unwrap the aluminum foil surrounding the pills. Finally, they were free. Cummings popped both hits of speed into his mouth and washed them down with the last remnants of the cold coffee.

It took ten minutes for him to get his clothes and boots back on. He flexed his fingers in an attempt to stimulate the circulation. They were tingling and felt slightly numb. He wrote it off to sleeping like a dead man in all the wrong positions. His bulging biceps hurt, and he had an occasional pain in the lower back. Despite the sleep, what little he'd had, Cummings still didn't feel rested. When he looked into the mirror to comb his thinning brown hair, he realized he looked just about as bad as he felt, like somebody had beaten him and left him for dead. But then that's what he paid the mamas for—to wear him completely out. He felt a certain sense of deep satisfaction knowing that the old gal who climbed into the sleeper last night had earned her money. And from what he could remember, she had been worth every dime of the forty bucks.

Cummings ran his tingling fingers through his thick brown beard. "Okay, Larry, baby, get your shit together and let's get truckin'."

He released the parking brake and dropped the Freightliner into gear. The clutch came out unsteadily, and the big rig leapt forward with a jerk. He dropped the clutch back to the floor and tapped on the accelerator in short, rapid strokes. The diesel engine perked back to life, and he let the clutch out once again, this time steadily and slowly.

The rig crept across the truck-stop parking lot until it reached the main roadway. Cummings looked both ways before he pulled onto the highway. That's when he realized his vision was blurred. Maybe it was from too much coke or not enough real rest, but whatever it was, he wasn't going to let it stop the delivery. He had, after all, driven with worse crud in his eyes when he had a summer head cold. No big deal.

The Freightliner was halfway into a left turn when Cummings heard the blaring car horn and screaming tires from behind him. He glanced into the rearview mirrors and saw a four-wheeler skidding sideways toward him. He reached up and yanked on the cord to sound the airhorn. It blared a loud warning, and then Cummings pressed harder on the accelerator. Once the rig was straightened out on the highway, he rolled the driver's window down, crammed his arm out, and shot the four-wheeler a finger. As he turned onto the entry ramp to Interstate 75, he mumbled something about how stupid four-wheeler drivers were.

At last the rig was rolling south on the superslab. If Lady Luck would park her sweet, tender loins on his dashboard, he could make up for lost time. If she didn't, then it was drivers beware, because Larry Cummings was hell-bound and determined to make the delivery on time. Seventy-eight thousand pounds of rolling thunder was going to cut a swatch across Ohio and back up to the docks right on schedule.

The big eighteen-wheeler rolled like a snowball going downhill for ten minutes. Nothing slowed it, nothing stopped it. But then the four-wheeler, driven by a pair of legs in a white miniskirt, cut sharply in front of the rig and stomped on the brakes for the next exit. Cummings stepped on the air breaks, and black smoke rolled from beneath the big rig. Burning rubber smeared into the pavement as the rig rocked and groaned.

The driver of the compact four-wheeler was oblivious to the nearly forty tons of steel machinery coming at her with the same lethal potential of a steam roller impacting an ant.

Cummings cursed loudly. "You crazy damned bitch!" He jerked hard to the left and narrowly missed the rear of the little compact car. The rig resisted the sudden turn by screaming and moaning with the sound of metal stressed to the threshold of disaster. At last Cummings regained control. He shook his head, trying to clear his vision. He looked ahead and scanned the traffic through his cloudy eyes. He took a deep breath and let it out. "Shit, man, damned four-wheelers. I sure could use a drink."

Cummings settled into the seat after he turned the audio level up on the console CB radio. He listened to the northbound eighteen-wheelers telling other southbound rigs about a major traffic tie-up twenty miles ahead in a construction zone. Although his fingers were still a little numb, he managed to draw a cigarette from his shirt pocket and get it lit. He took a soothing draw to calm his nerves. When he glanced at the speedometer, it was showing seventy-eight miles per hour. "All right, you highway menaces, I'm hammer down and comin' through town. Step on the gas or I'll run over your ass." Then he laughed so hard his head hurt.

"Come on, kids, get inside. Please stop fooling around. If you want to meet Daddy for lunch, we've got to hurry." Julie Foster shuffled her two children into the van like a mother hen rounding up baby chicks. Parenthood was her calling and all she had ever wanted. Right now she had it all.

Errin spoke first. "Mommy, where are we gonna meet Daddy?"

Before Julie could answer, Eric interrupted. "I want to go to McDonald's. Please, Mommy, can we go to McDonald's to eat?"

Julie warded off the parental frustration and forced a smile. "Now, listen. Let's all cooperate. We went to McDonald's last time, Eric. Today, Daddy wants us to meet him at the Captain's Fish Dock. We can't always live on hamburgers, you know."

Errin yelled. "Yeah! I love the Captain's fish and chips. Oh, boy, fries with lots of ketchup."

"Mommy, can I have shrimp? I love shrimp. And maybe some of that red stuff." Eric was jumping on the backseat and making no effort to conceal his happiness.

"Wait until we get there, Eric. You might change your mind."

"Oh, no, I won't. I like that red sauce and those pieces of lemon."

Errin made a silly face. "Mommy, don't let Eric eat those lemon slices in front of me. It makes my mouth feel funny when he does that. Yuk!"

Julie steered the van from the driveway and onto the quiet surburban street. "Errin, let him eat what he wants. If it bothers you, don't look at him."

Errin shot back, "Really, Mommy, it's yuk. How can he eat that stuff like that? I bet if I had a sister, she wouldn't eat lemon like that."

"Shut up, Errin. I'll eat it that way if I want to. Mommy just said I could. Didn't you, Mommy?"

Julie stopped the van at a stop sign. She looked carefully both ways and made a left turn. "Yes, Eric, I did. Now, both of you, calm down. Let's not be arguing when we pick Daddy up at the office. All right?"

Both kids nodded.

"Good. Now I want both of you to—"

Eric interrupted. "Are you sure we have to go to the fish place, Mommy? Can't we go to McDonald's?"

"No McDonald's today, Eric. It's definitely fish. I thought you liked the red sauce."

"Oh, I do, but I like the toys in the Happy Meals too. I was just checking to see if you'd changed your mind."

Julie almost laughed out loud. "No, Eric, I haven't changed my mind." She signaled her intention to turn onto the entry ramp to Interstate 75. She made the turn and accelerated out the ramp until she was in the flow of traffic. No sooner had she rounded the first curve on the four-lane highway than she had to decelerate— construction work ahead. Orange-and-white-striped plastic barrels lined the highway, forcing the four lanes into two slow-moving southbound lanes. And in front of her, cars coasted to a stop and blocked the highway.

Eric sensed the change and looked out the front windshield. "What's wrong, Mommy? Why are we stopping?"

"Traffic, darling. It's backed-up. Maybe I should have taken Carpenter Street instead of the outer loop."

Errin had to get a word in to ensure that Eric didn't have the opportunity to talk more than she did. "Are we going to be late for Daddy's lunch, Mommy?"

"No, Errin. It's still moving a little. We have enough time to get there. We can't be late for Daddy's lunch. This is a special occasion. He doesn't get the chance to do this every day. This is special."

Julie Foster glanced into the rearview mirror out of habit and saw forty tons of rolling death coming at her. In a double take, she thought her eyes were deceiving her.

Then, in a heartbeat, a weak, sickening feeling of helplessness rushed through her body. She knew there was no way the speeding tractor trailer could stop. It was traveling much too fast. Then she saw the vehicle skidding, sliding. The big truck was out of control and there was no way out. She knew it was going to crash into the van, and she had to do something to save the children. Out of fear and instinct, she screamed. "Oh, my God! Children, get down on the floor. He's going to hit us. Oh, God! Oh, no! David, I love you." The last thing Julie Foster heard before everything went dark and silent was the sound of metal tearing through metal and the children screaming. Then the van shook with a thunderous roar. It muffled the children's screams and fire was everywhere.

David Foster watched and listened. The veins in his temples protruded, but his face remained a work of stone. Expressionless. The words spoken by the minister were meaningless, and they flashed through his mind like fleeting strokes of lightning on some distant horizon. And the faces of relatives and friends . . . he scanned them, taking inventory one by one. He looked at them but didn't really *see* them. Tear, sobs, and sadness etched every face standing at the graveside . . . every face except his own. And now, three days into his new, lonely world, there were no more tears and no more emotions to be spilled from the fractured crevices of his heart.

The minister stopped talking, folded the Bible against his chest, and stepped away from the three coffins that would soon be lowered forever into the earth. David Foster stepped forward. He placed a single red rose on the first coffin, knelt, and gently kissed the vessel that would harbor a member of his family forever. He stood and repeated the process two more times. When he stood from the last coffin, he stepped away and stood beside a row of chairs that had been occupied by his closest living relatives and those of his wife.

The minister spoke with a saddened heart. "And so, dear God, we return these blessed, innocent souls into your coveted arms. And we ask that you keep them safely in your covenant until the time you choose to reunite this lovely family. And dear God, show those among the family and friends of these beloved deceased a way to understand and accept this horrible tragedy. And let the dust of these earthly bodies return to the dust of the earth from which they came. And take the innocent souls, dear God, to your heavenly home. Amen."

Slowly, the coffins decended silently into the cold ground. The people gathered at the graveside moved away in a procession of black-clad broken hearts. David Foster watched, the scene to be etched in his mind forever. His family, his life, everything he had ever known and loved, sank slowly into the ground before his eyes. And when the last coffin was laid to rest, he turned away.

For more than twenty minutes, people bade him condolences. He accepted their sympathy with dignity, but his mind was already at work.

Jerry Albertson, David's lifelong friend, stood beside him and held his arm. "Let's take a walk, David."

Foster turned and walked the way Albertson's arm guided him, away from the dispersing mourners.

"Where do you go from here, David?"

David Foster didn't answer for a long moment. He contemplated the question and looked into the overcast sky. "I don't know for sure, Jerry. I can't go back to the house, I know that much. Problem is, I have to. There are things I have to take care of."

Jerry could only imagine what David felt right now. "Listen, you're welcome to stay with Susie and me as long as you need to. I'm sure this is going to take some time to accept. My home is your home."

Foster pursed his lips and forced a smile he didn't feel. "My home just went into those three holes back there. My home, my life, everything. What does anything matter now? Some low-life bastard took it all away from me. What does it matter?"

Albertson couldn't think of a response. After a few moments, while the two men walked through the cemetery, he said, "The news said they released the truck driver from the hospital last night. They took him straight to jail. He's charged with three counts of vehicular homicide. They're going to hang his ass, David. The guy had drugs in his truck, and they found a high level in his system when they did the blood test. He'll never get out of jail. He'll pay for what he's done."

Foster felt the anger brewing inside of him. "Big deal. If he's convicted, he'll walk in eighteen months. You know how the system is. And they call it justice. He murdered my family, and he'll be free to do whatever he pleases in a few years. How about Julie and Errin and Eric . . . how free are they? Tell me that, Jerry . . . how long before they're free to walk around again?"

Albertson knew there was no answer. "Listen, David, you're not thinking what I think you're thinking, are you? I mean you're not going to do something stupid like try to get at this guy, are you?"

"No. Nothing I could do to him would ever bring my wife and my children back. He and I will both have to live with what he did. He was wrong. Going too fast, taking drugs, running forty tons of death like some hell-bent cowboy. I guess he was just trying to make a living the best way he knew. Guys like that, they never think about the consequences of what they do. They sit up there high above everything else on the highway like they own it, you know? Maybe some of the others like him will learn from this."

"Hey, David, all truck drivers aren't like that guy. He was one of the few. Most of 'em, they're family men like me and you." Albertson realized what he had said and shot back, "Oh, God, David, I'm sorry. I didn't mean . . ."

Foster looked at his friend's eyes. "Hey, it's okay. I understand."

"Really, David, this guy wasn't like most of 'em. A few rotten apples take drugs and drive like maniacs . . . it makes 'em all look bad. Look, I didn't mean to get into all this. Not now."

Foster walked to a headstone and stopped. He stared at the sky again. "I have the house up for sale. I did that last night. I'll go back there and get a few personal belongings. I don't know what after that. Everywhere I go, everything I do, I see them . . . all three of them. I wonder what fear they knew when the truck hit them and the fire—God, I can't even think about it. Oh, God, Jerry, it hurts." Foster dropped his head. The pain was there, but there were no more tears. They just wouldn't come.

Albertson tried to console his friend. "Don't you think that's a little premature? Give it some time, David."

"What time, Jerry? Where do I go in this town that I don't see their faces? What can I do that I'm not reminded of something we did as a family? There is no refuge here. I have to get away, go somewhere. I've got to."

Albertson released Foster's arm. "We've been friends a long time, David. I still think you're rushing it. What you're feeling is natural. You can't help but feel the hurt. But listen, old buddy, you can't quit living either. You got your whole life ahead of you. What are you now, thirty-three, thirty-four? You've got a great job and a lot of people who care about you. Don't quit on us."

"Believe me, Jerry, I'm not going to quit. No way."

Foster said good-bye to his friend, walked to the grave sites, and picked up a wreath of red roses. He knew it would always serve as a reminder of what had been and what was gone. He walked back to his car—brought there for him by another friend—and left the cemetery. He drove back to the house and forced himself to go inside. He sat there for an hour staring at a family portrait, and then he went to sleep.

He spent the next two weeks taking care of family business. He sold everything he could and donated what was left to GoodWill or the Salvation Army. He sold his Honda Accord and took that and the insurance check from the van and bought a new Chevrolet Blazer, a Honda 4 x 4 All Terrain Vehicle, and a tote trailer to haul it. He bought a cabin tent and a large assortment of camping gear. And his gun collection, most of which he'd sold to a local gun shop. In return for a dozen assorted sporting arms, he took a Ruger Mini-14 .223 assault rifle, a case of ammunition, a Ruger GP-100 .357 Magnum, and a Ruger .22 automatic.

On the third week after the tragedy, David Foster loaded the Chevy Blazer with everything he could carry and everything he thought he might need. He filled the Blazer with gasoline and headed out on the open road.

He had taken the life insurance payoffs and converted them into cashier's checks, which he carried with the proceeds of the household inventory sale in a brown manila envelope. The proceeds from the destruction of his life totaled more than three hundred thousand dollars. Foster had decided to open an account in some small town far away from everything he had ever known. He had given notice to his employer that he would take his vacation time and then he wouldn't be back. All of the loose ends were tied neatly—credit cards canceled, accounts closed, obligations settled. There was nothing to keep him tied down or restrict his travel. He thumbed through his newly acquired atlas and landed on northern Arkansas—the Ozarks.

Foster spent a few minutes plotting his travel to the mountains. He calculated the time and the mileage, realizing that old habits of thorough planning died hard.

He put the Blazer in gear and pulled onto the highway. When he left the city limits of his home town behind, David Foster effectively disappeared from the face of the earth . . . from everything he had ever known and anyone who had ever known him.

Chapter Two

1990

Marc Lee leafed through the truckers' magazine. A short news article caught his eye, and he stopped long enough to read it. "Hey, Carl, come have a look at this."

Carl Browne sat his coffee down and walked across the truckstop lounge to where Marc was sitting. "What did you find?"

"This." Marc pointed to the article in the magazine. "Take a look."

Carl took the magazine and read the short article. "Interesting. Three dead truck drivers in less than two months. All of 'em at rest areas and all of 'em carrying drugs in the cabs. Competition?"

"I don't know. They're all in different parts of the country. Besides the fact that they're all dead and there were drugs, there doesn't seem to be a common link. But then, there's not a lot to go on in this article. It does sound like something is amiss."

Carl handed the magazine back to Marc. "Might be worth checking into once we're back in Dallas. Maybe Brittin could do some preliminaries for us before we get back to Leeco. Speaking of which, you about ready to hit the road?"

Marc tossed the magazine back onto the table in front of him and got up from his seat. "Yep, let's do it."

The Delta Force warriors, turned Highway Warriors, left the truckstop lounge and walked outside to their high-tech Leeco overroad rig in the truck parking area. They climbed aboard the big eighteen-wheeler and headed for the highway.

The giant Caterpillar 1400-horsepower diesel power plant in the custom rig hummed a wistful tune as Marc shifted through the gears. The engine, like almost everything else on the technically advanced overroad rig, was custom designed especially for the Leeco rig by special presidential order. The designers had taken advantage of the latest technology to create a highly reliable and functional power plant that occupied little more space than a standard Cat diesel engine.

Since the inception of the president's top secret project to combat the hordes of criminal scumbags that cluttered America, the overroad rig had proven itself a highly functional piece of fighting equipment. And, to date, the president of the United States had been very pleased with the results of his sixteen-million-dollar investment.

The war on crime raged on. Many battles had been won, but there remained many to be fought before the country was once again really free and safe for its inhabitants. The scourge was rampant, and the doers of evil still filled the headlines with their horrid deeds. And the president was even more commited now than he had been at the outset of the violent war. The slime must be reduced and the vermin extinguished so that innocent, decent people, could once again feel safe in the Land of the Free. Lawlessness was all too prevalent, and those who broke the laws of the land for the sake of greed enjoyed more rights than their victims. And that was the reason the president took his courageous step and jeopardized the sanctity of the very office he held: to stop the bacteria before it devoured the heart and soul of the American population.

Marc Lee and Carl Browne were the point men in the raging war. And from where they sat, there appeared to be no end in sight. All too often, the biased liberal news media portrayed the perpetrating criminal as more the victim than those whose lives he had ravaged. The country had evolved into a mockery of human rights and solid values. Even the United States Supreme Court had diluted the true intent of the laws of the land to such a degree that protestors openly burned the American flag with no fear of retribution.

As Marc drove, he thought of the thousands of American men who had fought and died for the sake of the flag. He thought especially of the men who at Iwo Jima had given their lives to see the mighty Stars and Stripes fly over that embattled Japanese hill. And in Vietnam, the countless souls, the sons of American families, who had been mortally wounded at places like Hamburger Hill. And the list went on and on. But today, to permit the rape of the entire country by permitting the public sacrilege of flag burning as a guaranteed First Amendment right seemed a nauseating reminder of the *real* state of American affairs.

The country had evolved into a land where use of mind-altering drugs was as commonplace as driving a car. The war was made more difficult because the people who were elected by the population to protect rights, make laws, and secure the enforcement to the advantage of the common man, had themselves become users of the very drugs they sought to obliterate. The tentacles ran too deep and the seed of deceit was too deeply sown into the American culture. But win or lose, the Highway Warriors fought on.

Carl broke the silence. "You look like you're deep in thought over there."

Marc kept his eyes on the road ahead. "Yeah, I guess I was."

"What were you thinking?"

"About the reason we're doing all of this. About scumbags and drugs. The way things are."

Carl shrugged his shoulders. "All we can do is put our own dent in it. I'm not convinced we can ever stop it."

"I think you're right about that. I've said for years that America's freedom is destroying her. Do you understand that?"

"Yeah, man, I understand. You and me, our families, we're living proof of the way things are. This is the greatest country on earth, and politicians and a handful of lawyers are taking it down the sewer."

Marc relaxed his hands on the steering wheel of the big overroad rig. "Did you ever stop and think what people like Thomas Jefferson would think if they could come back today and see what they'd created? I can't help but believe what we have today in this country isn't exactly what those brave men had in mind when they jeopardized their very lives and declared American independence. If even the toughest among them— Washington, Jefferson, Madison, Monroe, Franklin— could see it today, they'd probably throw up first, then sit down and cry."

The sound of a blaring electronic siren took the Warriors' attention off of the conversation. A red BMW passed the rig at high speed. Directly behind it, a highway patrol car was in pursuit. Marc moved the rig into the deceleration lane on the shoulder to give the police car plenty of room to pass.

Carl jerked his head around and followed the speeding vehicles with his eyes. "What the hell you reckon that's all about?"

"We can follow and find out." Marc stepped on the accelerator and increased the overroad rig's speed.

The BMW and the patrol car disappeared over a hill just ahead. Marc kept the rig moving fast. The giant diesel engine moved the heavy Leeco war machine with ease. The rig topped the hill, and on the other side, a long, steep grade dropped into the valley below. At the bottom of the long grade, another pair of blue lights flashed, and the speeding BMW was headed straight for it.

Carl spoke first. "The shit's gonna fly in just a minute. Smokie's waitin' on the dude."

No sooner had the words cleared his mouth, than black smoke rose from the highway far in front of the Leeco rig at the bottom of the hill. The BMW was in a broadside, the highway patrol car directly behind it. Then, from the clouds of heavy rubber smoke, the BMW appeared, but now it was heading in the opposite direction—straight for the Leeco rig.

Carl shouted. "Look at that crazy son of a bitch. He's going the wrong way on an interstate highway. He's nuts."

The highway patrol car reappeared. It too was traveling in the wrong direction and headed straight for the rig.

Marc braked hard and slowed the rig. The oncoming cars were less than a quarter of a mile away and traveling at high speeds. Marc turned from the right lane and settled the rig across the highway at a forty-five degree angle. "Hang on, we're about to see what that asshole is made of."

"I'm holdin'," Carl said as he reached beneath his shirt and came out with his Smith & Wesson 5906 9mm automatic.

The rig stopped, effectively blocking the road. On each side of the sloping roadway, there were high embankments. The driver of the BMW had one of two choices: stop or collide with the huge eighteen-wheeler.

The BMW was closer now, and Marc could see two men in the front seat. He could also see the panic in their eyes. And behind them, the patrol car gained ground. Then, the BMW went into another slide. More black smoke rolled as the driver tried to spin the car around. Behind him, the second patrol car was gaining momentum. Suddenly, both police cars skidded sideways and screamed to a stop. The roadway was blocked, and the BMW driver had no way out. He stopped the vehicle midway between the Leeco rig and the highway patrol cars. He sat idle for a long moment. The two state troopers jumped from their cars and came down with riot shotguns. One of them held a microphone in his hand.

The air filled with sound from a blaring PA system. "You in the BMW, step from the vehicle and lie face down on the pavement with your arms and legs spread. Do it now!"

The BMW's driver let the car move slightly forward. He turned sideways to the patrol cars, and both men jumped from the driver's side. They took cover from the troopers. In their hands were handguns.

The PA blared again. "This is your last chance. You have no escape. Throw down your weapons and surrender."

One of the men from the BMW answered the trooper's demands with gunfire. Five or six shots rang out. Then came a shotgun blast from one of the troopers. Marc looked hard at the troopers. One of them was missing, the other held his shotgun steadily and crouched behind the fender well of the patrol car.

More shots. The BMW shooters fired hard and fast at the patrol car and the remaining trooper.

Marc reached behind the driver's seat in the big rig for his silenced Uzi 9mm submachine gun. "Looks like that trooper could use some help."

Carl did the same thing. "Let's bail him out. His partner must be hit."

Marc switched on the Leeco rig's PA system and picked up the microphone. "You in the BMW. Do what the trooper said. Drop your weapons."

The shooters appeared stunned to hear the sound coming from a tractor-trailer rig. One of them turned around and fired two fast shots into the front of the rig. The bullets impacted the Armorshield body armor of the rig and evaporated.

Carl laughed. "Dumbasses!"

Marc opened his door and climbed from the rig. Carl followed, exiting on the driver's side for cover.

The trooper wasn't sure what was going on. He laid low, watching over the barrel of his shotgun.

Carl moved to the back of the rig and to the right side behind the rear axle. He took cover and then took aim. He yelled. "Okay, dipshit. Lay those guns down or your asses are history."

———

David Foster stepped out of the cabin door and took a deep breath of the fresh mountain air. He stretched his arms and looked around the small clearing that surrounded his secluded retreat. His home. Compared to the modern suburban house he had left behind two years ago when his family had died suddenly and tragically, the cabin was a mere shack. But now, to David Foster, it was his solitude and his refuge.

When he had first entered the Ozarks on his mission of escape, Foster had no intention of becoming a hermit. The solitude and the tranquility he had found high up in the mountains had helped him accept the sudden death of his wife and two children. From the cool morning air and the language of the forests at night came an inner peace the thirty-six-year-old former credit manager had never known. Armed with an aching heart from one of life's regrettable twists, Foster had escaped and then withdrawn from the society and culture he had known his entire life.

Each passing day helped him adapt to his surroundings. He had become one with the mountains and the forests. He had learned to live off the bounty of the land. The first winter had been harsh, and there were times, particularly at night, when he'd thought he would freeze to death and never be found by another human being. The tent he had purchased before he left the city had provided little shelter from the bitter winter winds and the snows that fell almost constantly. His reserve supply of Mountain House freeze-dried food had deplenished faster than he had anticipated. Once the food was gone, Foster faced critical choices: He could leave the mountains and go back to civilization, or he could stay and adapt to his environment. He had, out of a need for isolation, chosen the latter.

Since his withdrawal from city life, Foster had left the mountains on only five occasions. Two of those trips were for supplies and three for the purpose of his mission. He had brought with him a large supply of ammunition for his weapons. He had never been proficient with any type of rifle or handgun, but days upon days spent practicing and learning had changed all of that. He was now an incredible marksman. Time and patience had honed the instinctive hunting skills that are harbored within the souls of most men. The ability to hunt, track, and exist among the creatures of the high mountain forests had evolved from almost non-existent to that of a seasoned mountain man.

David Foster didn't regret leaving the scourge of society behind him. He didn't miss time schedules, ringing telephones, bills in the mail, or headline news items about drug-crazed maniacs. No, here in the mountains, he made his own schedule to coincide with nature, and the only alarm clock was an occasional blue jay squawking at sunrise over the eastern ridges. More than anything else, the solitude of the mountains gave David Foster time to think and plan.

Two years earlier, when the drugged-out truck driver had annihilated his family, Foster thought the world had ended. Faced with the reality of haunting memories confronting him at every turn, he had chosen to leave it all behind and find a new reality. And the mountains gave him that. The clean-shaven businessman he had once been became a bearded master of basic survival. He had served two years in the army prior to seeking his master's degree in business administration. During those two years he had learned the basic elements of survival and self-protection against man-made elements. Among the few books he had taken when he left were manuals he had retained from his military days. And now, alone against nature, he found those manuals had become his bibles, guiding and teaching him.

The isolated mountain home was built on government land high in the Ozark Mountains of northern Arkansas. During the past two years, he had neither seen nor heard another human being except when he went down to replenish supplies or accomplish the mission. Foster suspected he could live out the remainder of his life without ever encountering another living soul. And that suited him just fine.

Days were spent building the rough cabin from the resources so abundant in the high country. He had designed his shelter to be both functional and comfortable. Each log used to frame the outer walls had to be harvested from the hardwood timber. The first trees to form the shell of the cabin had come from the area he cleared for his new home. A small fast-flowing mountain stream ran near the cabin. The native trout that dwelled there had provided nourishment. His angling abilities were lacking at first, but out of necessity he had become quite proficient at catching the elusive fish.

Winter heat came from two stone fireplaces, one at each end of the cabin. Naturally dried oak had been sculptured into a table and crude chairs. Most of the woodwork was done with a simple saw, an ax, a hatchet, and his Buckmaster knife.

On one of his visits to civilization, he had purchased a sufficient quantity of PVC pipe to divert water from the stream into his cabin. A large hollowed-out log formed his kitchen sink, and a simple T-tap valve provided the luxury of running water. A pile of rocks rose from the ground outside to a level of four or five feet. Atop them, a fire pit lay beneath a salvaged fifty-five-gallon barrel he had acquired at the time he purchased the PVC pipe.

When he wanted a shower, he simply built a fire under the barrel and heated the water. When he was satisfied with the temperature, he turned the water on and allowed it to flow by gravity to a makeshift shower head. It wasn't as luxurious as the fancy bathroom he had when Julie was alive, but it was cheaper to operate.

It had taken eight months to build the cabin. Foster had found resources within himself that he never dared to imagine as he confronted each day of construction. He had secured the perimeter one hundred yards in every direction with a series of military-style booby traps. Any intrusion by man would be detected instantly. If, after detection, Foster deemed the intruder a threat, then a secondary battery of traps could be activated that would render the intruder immobile or dead.

Food was plentiful in the mountains. Resourcefulness yielded an abundance of nourishment. There was always fresh meat for the taking. Fish, nuts, berries, and roots were plentiful. Foster had cultivated a small garden for summer vegetables and dried winter storage. When he longed for something more conventional, he would break out one of the freeze-dried food packets he had purchased on his visits back to mankind.

An advantage he hadn't excepted was the return of his eyesight. For years he had worn glasses to read. And now, after so much time in the purity of his new surroundings, he had found the glasses unnecessary. The phenomenon had amazed him, but he didn't bother to question it because the improved eyesight served to strengthen his abilities for the mission.

Foster had taken the money from the sale of his life's work and deposited it in five small banks in northern Arkansas and southern Missouri. At each bank, he had used a fictitious name and social security number. The money was for a major emergency, and at this point in his life, it really didn't mean anything to him. He kept it for the remote chance that someday he might decide to go back to society and live.

Foster finished his morning survey of his home. Everything looked fine. Once back inside the cabin, he prepared himself a special treat—freeze-dried scrambled eggs and country cured ham that he had purchased after the last mission. When breakfast was done, he gathered his backpack and accessories. He grabbed the Ruger Mini-14 from the handhewn fireplace hearth and checked the chamber. As usual it was empty. He slipped a Federal Ordinance 30-round magazine into the well and drew the bolt lever back. When it slammed shut, a 52-grain hollow-point round filled the chamber.

Next came the Ruger Mark II .22 automatic. With a round chambered in that, he slid it into the backpack. When the Buckmaster survival knife cleared its sheath, Foster ran his finger across the edge to make sure it was ready for service. It was. He left the cabin and mounted the Honda 4 x 4 ATV for the long ride to his Chevy Blazer.

The ride took thirty minutes of weaving and threading through the heavy forests. When he reached the Blazer, he found it just as he always had—secure and unmolested beneath a cover of underbrush. Another ten minutes passed while David Foster cleared the brush away. He loaded his backpack and the Mini-14 inside and got in. At the first tap of the starter, the Chevy engine growled as if it wasn't going to start. On the second try it caught and the engine rumbled.

Foster drove from the laurel grove and stopped the Chevy. He went back and moved the Honda to where the Chevy had been and covered it securely.

He drove the Chevy from the mountain and headed for the interstate highway near Fort Smith, Arkansas. It was time for another mission, and when he returned to the mountain several days from now, another drugged-out truck driver would be lying dead as just payment for his indiscretion. And that would be one less menace on the highway to kill some innocent family.

Chapter Three

Glen Hawthorn wanted to get on the road. He sat in the tiny driver's lounge while the dock workers finished loading his trailer. A glance at his watch told him he would have to hammer-down hard if he was going to make Fort Smith before midafternoon. The ride from Oklahoma City to western Arkansas was long and tedious, but that's what he was paid to do. Besides, after Fort Smith, it was back to Dallas and home for at least a week.

Hawthorn had driven an eighteen-wheel overroad rig for slightly over ten years, and the one part he had never gotten used to was the waiting. Waiting to load and then waiting to be unloaded. But, like speed cops and weigh stations, it came with the turf. He found the time useful to catch up on his paperwork, and when that was completed, he usually read some newspaper or a Louis L'Amour novel. The newspapers kept him abreast with what was happening in the world while he traveled, and the novels kept him in a fantasy world when he needed an escape from the real one. Either way, the waiting never seemed to end. And worse than anything, when the dock workers were behind he was forced to take a lot of chances on the highway in order to make up for the time lost sitting on his backside.

Despite the hours of waiting in tiny lounges like the one he sat in now and despite truckstop coffee, speed cops, and weigh stations, Hawthorn didn't want any other way of life. No, trucking was the only way to go. Because for all the boring hours and frustrating dock workers, there were other hours and other faces along the highways that made up for the slack. Driving an eighteen-wheel truck took him to places in America that other, work-a-day people could only dream of. And then there were the places so carved in beauty that those who spent their time working in factories or offices never had time to see. So waiting and dodging the bears was the bitter, but the scenery and the experiences along America's highways was the sweet. All in all it totaled more sweet than bitter for the modern-day nomad-at-heart.

Truth was, there wasn't a great deal of difference between what he did for a living in the 1990s and what a true-blooded American cowboy did in the 1880s. They were both guidance systems for delivery of goods to the common market. Where the cowboy had made his long haul running cattle to market along the plains, the trucker ran his cargo to the modern market by running the blacktop and concrete plains called highways. They both spent a lot of long, lonely nights beneath the same moon and suffered through hot days under the same sun. And when their toil was done, they had delivered the goods and were compensated accordingly. Both were frequently gone from their families for weeks or months, and the familiarity of their homes lived only in their memories. All for the sake of making a living. And somewhere along the way, both had made a choice for their nomadic existence.

Two days from now, back home in Dallas, this run would be over. And for a while, Hawthorn knew he'd settle into the comfort of his real home instead of the one with eighteen-wheels under it. In the meantime, it was full concentration on the way he made his living, and that meant carefully rolling eighteen-wheels over white-striped blacktop and concrete while making up the excess time at the terminal.

The dock foreman's voice returned Glen Hawthorn from his self-imposed trance. "Hawthorn, you're loaded and ready to roll."

Hawthorn stood from the lounge sofa and went to the dock. "Is she buttoned down?"

The crass dock foreman made a disgusted face. "Hey, I said you're ready to roll, didn't I? She's loaded and sealed. Sign on the line and get the hell away from my dock. I got freight to move."

Hawthorn stared at the guy. "That's what I like about you, Albert, you're loaded with personality. Guys like you make my job so pleasant."

"Bite it, Hawthorn. Sign the sheet and get moving."

Hawthorn signed for the load and handed the paperwork back to Albert. "See you in a couple of weeks, Speedy. You need to get laid or something. Your attitude sucks."

Albert spit into his Styrofoam cup that had been converted into a spitoon. "Get your ass out of here, Hawthorn, before I kick it. You're holding up progress."

Glen Hawthorn left the dock and went to his overroad rig. He made a walk-around inspection. Everything looked okay, so he climbed aboard and fired the Cat diesel engine. He drove away from the dock and headed to the last stop before home—Fort Smith, Arkansas.

Thirty minutes out on the highway, Hawthorn realized his sinuses were killing him. He fumbled through his black travel bag and found the prescription medication the doctor in Dallas had given him. He popped the top off and dumped two of the multicolored capsules onto his lap. He managed to get the top back on with one hand. When he was finished, he found the remains of a Pepsi sitting on the console. One quick swoop of the hand and the two capsules of miracle drug—guaranteed not to cause drowsiness—landed in his mouth. He washed them down with the Pepsi and returned his attention to the road.

He took the brown pill bottle and glanced at it through the windshield light. Only four capsules remained. If he was frugal, that would be enough to get him home where the bottle could be refilled. If he wasn't frugal, odds were his sinuses would kill him.

———

The shooters beside the BMW paid no attention to Carl's warning. Two or three shots came fast in the direction of Carl and the Leeco rig.

Carl held his fire. He looked hard at the men with the guns. They were inescapably trapped and obviously too foolish or too scared to realize it. "Okay, assholes, this is it. Last chance. Lay those guns down and spread eagle!"

The shooters answered with more gunfire.

At the front of the Leeco rig, Marc had taken his defensive pattern. He couldn't see the state trooper from where he was, but he knew Carl could. He flicked the selector on the Uzi and made ready to send hellfire toward the two men who had been running from the law. He yelled at the men, "Give it up. You're surrounded. There's nowhere for you to go except to hell if you don't surrender."

More gunfire, and the first shooter, the one shorter than the second man, scrambled to change magazines in his empty automatic pistol. The second shooter moved around and ducked beside the BMW like a frightened chicken. He turned suddenly toward Marc and fired a shot.

Marc came on line with the Uzi, and his finger eased back on the trigger. A shotgun blast from the trooper changed his intentions when the second man hit the ground and rolled.

The shooter was up, running at the state police car like a crazed, suicidal maniac. The automatic pistol in his hands spit rapid flashes of death in the direction of the trooper.

Marc moved from his position to the opposite side of the armored Leeco rig. He came down on the second man with the Uzi.

Another shotgun blast, and the armed bad man tumbled to the pavement. The trooper racked the empty out of his shotgun and crammed another into the spout. But then, like a killing machine, the downed shooter was up. He ran hard, stumbling and firing at the same time.

A shot got lucky and the remaining state trooper fell from view. Then, from nowhere, he appeared at the trunk of the car. He leaned across and fired another blast from the riot shotgun. This time, the shooter took the full load in the chest and crashed violently to the pavement.

The trooper was moving again, to the front of his car. He jacked another load into the shotgun and searched for the second man from the BMW.

The second man had reloaded. He faced the trooper and fired twice. Both shots missed. He looked over his shoulder, toward the Leeco rig, and fired another shot in the direction of Carl at the rear of the rig. That shot also went wild and slammed harmlessly into the Armorshield surface of the rig.

Carl rolled onto the pavement into a prone position and tapped off a three-round burst to divert the man's attention. The shots peppered the body of the BMW, and the shooter hit the pavement.

Then, like a raging bull, the shooter came from the pavement and scrambled into the driver's seat of the BMW. He started the engine and spun around, headed straight for the trooper's car.

Marc and Carl moved at the same time. Both Highway Warriors were on their feet. Their silenced Uzis spat hellfire toward the fleeing car. Multiple 9mm rounds slammed into the car's body.

The BMW was out of control and gaining speed as it headed on a course of destruction. Hot 9mm slugs chewed through metal. Shards of broken safety glass littered the highway, but the vehicle didn't slow down.

The trooper saw what was inevitable and leaped for safety. No sooner had he rolled into the gravel at the edge of the pavement, than the speeding BMW crashed into both police cars. Debris rained skyward from the impact and then fell back to the ground amid the tangled wreckage.

Cars were stopping now behind the Leeco rig. Drivers curious to see the cause of the delay stepped from their cars.

Marc and Carl moved toward the wrecked vehicles. They were thirty feet away from the smashed BMW when the driver's door suddenly flew open and the shooter, blood streaming from his face, jumped out onto the pavement. His automatic pistol was in his right hand. The man stumbled, obviously dazed from the brutal impact, and then fired in the direction of the Warriors.

Marc rolled left to the pavement and Carl rolled right. The shooter tried to select a target, but he was too rattled from the collision. Finally, in a move of desperation, he settled the automatic in Carl's direction. Two rapid shots rang out and sent chips of pavement flying.

Carl covered his eyes from the spray of splattering lead and blacktop. He dumped two quick three-round bursts toward the shooter, more for cover fire than an attempt to hit the guy.

Then the shooter was running, stumbling. He ran straight toward the Leeco rig, between Marc and Carl.

The trooper was back on his feet now, scrambling for cover and a look at what was unfolding on the highway.

Ten feet away from the BMW, the dazed shooter stopped and ran back toward his totaled car. He fired two more shots; both went wild into the sky.

Marc and Carl searched for a clear shot, one that, should it miss, wouldn't chance hitting the trooper or the crashed vehicles because now the smell of gasoline leaking onto the highway was pungent. And that made the situation even more volatile. A stream of hot lead into the wrong place, and the highway would erupt into a raging fireball. And should the fireball cleanse the highway of the dirtbag with the gun, then so be it. But it didn't stop there, because Marc, Carl, and the state trooper were all too close to escape safely.

The dirtbag reached inside the crashed BMW and grabbed an attaché case. Once he had it safely in his hands, he ran hard toward the Leeco rig.

Marc was the first to yell. "Stop!"

The shooter answered with gunfire.

Marc and Carl opened fire. The Uzis sang a death chant, and the shooter was stopped cold in his tracks. He hung there, suspended by some unknown force, twitching rhythmically, for a long moment. He fired the automatic pistol as another volley of 9mm justice tore through him. His body's muscular reactions caused the automatic in his hand to fire on the way to the ground. Finally, the pistol lay silent beside the evil hand that had held it. The man's other hand was wrapped around the handle of the attaché case in a death grip.

The Warriors were up and running at almost the same time. Carl reached the fallen man first. He kicked the pistol away from the man's hand and then knelt beside the still body. His left hand went to the juglar for a pulse. As expected, there was none. Highway justice at its best had prevailed. Carl looked up at Marc. "This sack of shit's finished."

Marc looked at the bloody body when he stopped beside Carl. "Crazy son of a bitch. I couldn't tell what the guy was gonna do from one second to the next. He had to be on something. He wouldn't go down. Like he was a zombie or something inhuman."

Carl stayed down on one knee. "Wonder what this was all about."

The trooper had left the cover of the tangled wreckage now. He had run toward Marc and Carl, and his shotgun was leveled at them. "Open that case and I expect you'll see what this was all about. Until you do, lay those weapons down very gently. I don't know who or what you guys are, but you've got some tall explaining to do about those machine guns you're carrying."

The Warriors looked at each other and then at the trooper. The trooper's eyes were locked onto the machine-gun-toting men. No one noticed the first shooter from the BMW as he fumbled to his knees behind them.

———

David Foster watched the white lines move past him on the highway. Each broken line took him one step closer to the project that now consumed his life. The Chevy Blazer ate the highway as the miles churned by toward Fort Smith. This would be the fourth mission in as many months. This time, unlike the previous outings, Foster was determined to reach his ultimate target.

Russellville, Arkansas, was just ahead. Foster re-worked his plans mentally, just like before. He spotted the small strip shopping center and turned in. He parked near a twenty-four-hour restaurant and shut the Blazer down.

It took ten minutes to gather everything he in-tended to take on the trip, and when that was done, he climbed from the Blazer and locked it. As he walked across the parking lot, a satisfied smile crossed his face. But the smile left as quickly as it had come when a mental picture filled his brain—three caskets drifting slowly into the cold ground.

Foster reached the highway and walked toward Interstate 40, a half-mile away. When he reached the entry ramp, he set his backpack down on the ground at his feet and hoisted his thumb high into the air. He knew it wouldn't be long before someone offered him, the weary hitchhiker, a ride. And unless it was a trucker, his excuses for refusing the ride were already lined up because this hitchhiker only wanted truckers.

He saw a rig heading for the ramp. His thumb remained high as he tried to slow the big eighteen-wheeler. The driver didn't stop, but David Foster wasn't worried because soon one would.

David Foster looked more like a refugee from the late 1960s. He wore his hair long and stringy. He hadn't shaved since he couldn't remember when, and the beard that grew over his hardened face was scraggly and painted with streaks of gray. His denim jeans were worn and faded from hours in the mountains. A flannel shirt was unbuttoned to the third button underneath his GoreTex camouflage jacket, which exposed the hair on his chest. His feet walked in the comfort of a broken-in pair of Browning hiking boots. The backpack that provided for all the comforts of home that Foster desired was one of the fancy type with the rigid aluminum frame, the kind usually found in some elite outdoor outfitter's shop. He had a tattered sleeping bag attached to the bottom of the pack frame with two flexible straps. On the side of the pack was a blanketed two-quart canteen filled with water.

On the outside, David Foster looked like any one of the hundreds of hikers seen across America every day, a man wandering aimlessly trying to "find himself" or discover America. But on the inside, David Foster wasn't trying to find himself. He was trying to find Larry Cummings. Like so many other hiking travelers, his journey wasn't an aimless one because David Foster had a mission.

The first decent from the mountains had come after eleven months in solitude. Foster had used that trip as a seek and discover mission. He had very quietly traced the chronicles of the driver who had destroyed his family and his own life. And he hadn't been surprised at what he had found. The driver had been convicted of three counts of involuntary manslaughter and sentenced to three years in prison on each count. The sentences were imposed to run concurrently so after only fifteen months in correctional confinement, the driver was a free man. That translated into only five months from the first trek from the mountains, give or take a month for the judicial proceedings.

The discovery of the sentence renewed the rage Foster had felt but kept hidden at the time of the tragedy. It also renewed his determination to seek a remedy that matched the crime. Simply put, death.

When Foster returned to the mountains, he had brought along a box of books. One that soon became his favorite was a home medical remedy and chemical book along the lines of *The Poor Man's James Bond*. In that publication, Foster found numerous compositions that could be formulated from resources of the natural environment. Some had served him well during minor illnesses, and others struck possibilities for use on his mission.

Foster had spent countless hours reading and re-reading the books. He had renewed his knowledge of survival against the elements, fortification of a retreat, unconventional warfare, and basic chemistry. He had reread it so many times, in fact, that he had virtually memorized the books and manuals. But not satisfied with mere rote, he committed the knowledge to memory until it became second nature. And now, two years after the death of his family, David Foster felt competent as a combatant and a survivor.

Aside from the construction of his mountain home, Foster had taken the newly acquired knowledge and practiced it every day for months. He had transformed David Foster the citified, complacent credit manager into David Foster the keen, astute survival machine. He had brought to life the cunning and determination that had lain dormant within him as they do in most men. And when he had found those elements inside himself, he had honed them to surgical precision by raw desire and daily use. Aside from the long hair, the beard, and the conspicuously absent coat and tie, David Foster on the outside looked no different from anyone else. But on the inside his razor-sharp mind was dedicated to a mission.

He saw another eighteen-wheeler turn onto the ramp. The thumb instinctively went high, and Foster assumed the most tranquil look he could. The roaring diesel engine wound down and the eighteen-wheeler slowed. The trucker pulled the rig to the side of the road ahead of Foster and switched on his four-way blinkers.

Foster grabbed his backpack and ran for the passenger's side of the rig. He climbed up on the step and opened the door. A bearded trucker's face greeted him.

The trucker sat half-leaning on the steering wheel. "Where you headed, dude?"

Foster returned the greeting. "Fort Smith and all points south."

"Hop in. Next stop is Fort Smith."

"Thanks." Foster climbed inside the Kenworth cab and stowed his backpack. "I was beginning to wonder if I would be on that ramp all day."

"It's the beard. People get scared of guys on the side of the road with a beard. My name's Hazelwood. Ronnie Hazelwood. What's yours?"

"I'm Donald Puckett. Nice to make your acquaintance." Foster leaned over and shook hands with the driver.

"Hey, believe me, it's the beard. I get shit all the time about mine. I figure it ain't nobody's business 'cept mine so I don't pay a lot of attention to it. What you got happening in Fort Smith? That is, if you don't mind me askin'."

"Hey, man, no problem. I'm thankful to get a ride. Wow. Fort Smith. Well, I'll tell you the truth, I got to get another ride there. I think I'll go south for a while. Won't be long till winter sets in up this way. Gets colder than a witch's tit around here, so I'm told. Where you headed?"

"Albuquerque and then back to Miami. You been waitin' long?"

"No, not long. Maybe an hour. Hey, Russellville looks like a strange little town for you to be stoppin' in. You takin' a whiz or what?"

The driver laughed. "You're hip, ain't you, man? I mean, you look like you're hip. Am I right?"

Foster returned the laugh. "Yeah, man, I'm cool. Why?"

"Well, Russellville ain't on my schedule, you see. I got this chick here I met a long time back. The nookie's pretty decent and I always score me some speed whenever I pass through. Kind of a double treat, you know what I mean?"

Foster laughed hard. "You're a sly one all right. Shit, I didn't know you guys like to get high."

"Oh, don't get me wrong, it ain't a habit. I like some good shit once in a while. I like to blow a little pot to help me float over the concrete. And the speed, well, it makes it a lot easier to drive all night, and it's nothin' I couldn't get from a doctor if I had time. Nothin' heavy, though. I ain't into drugs. You know what I mean?"

Foster settled back into the seat and got comfortable. "Hey, man, I can dig it. Live it like you see it, I always say."

The driver had the rig on the highway now and moved with the traffic flow on I-40 westbound. "You look like a man who's tripped a time or two. What's your favorite score?"

Foster was totally relaxed now because Lady Luck had smiled on him. He had his own double bonus: a ride and a druggie. "I like the designer stuff, myself. Nothin' hard, nothin' heavy, just the ultimate mellow. Makes grass seem like tokin' on a candy cigarette. If you're hip, I'll lay a hit on you the next time we stop."

The driver pressed on the accelerator. "Sounds cool, man. I love mellow."

Chapter Four

Marc stared hard into the trooper's eyes. "Look, we're on your side. You'd better get over there and check on your fallen comrade instead of worrying about us."

The trooper was undaunted. "He's dead. Took one right in the face. I certainly hope ballistics will confirm that it was one of theirs and not one of yours. Just so we can find out, lay those weapons down."

Marc stared into the barrel of the lawman's shotgun and then his eyes went beyond the gun. Movement. "Behind you! Get down!"

The trooper didn't have time to react. Carl was already moving, airborne. He struck the lawman and the shotgun broadside. The impact of the huge Highway Warrior knocked the trooper off balance. He stumbled and fell to the road just as a single shot rang out from behind him.

The shooter who had fallen first was stumbling to his feet. He had the handgun poised and aimed toward Marc, Carl, and the trooper.

Marc immediately rolled right when Carl hit the trooper's shotgun. He slammed into the pavement and rolled two or three turns. When he came out of the roll, his Uzi sent silent flying death pellets toward the shooter. The 115-grain jacketed hollow points riveted the shooter's chest. The man spun around from the impact, but he didn't go down.

The shooter regained his balance and half-ran, half-stumbled toward one of the wrecked patrol cars.

Marc got the picture quickly. A ballastic vest. He squeezed the Uzi's trigger and made a sweeping figure-eight with the flaming muzzle. This time, a full-auto barrage caught the shooter in the neck and head. The impact sent blood and fragments into the air in a crimson spray. The shooter trembled like he was entranced by a seizure and then plummeted to the ground. When his dead gun-bearing hand slapped the pavement, a single shot rang out. The bullet went wild and ricocheted off the road's surface before slamming into the body of the crashed BMW.

That's all it took. A spray of sparks met with one of several streams of gasoline from the crashed vehicles. In a microinstant after the shot resonated overhead, a brilliant flash filled the air and flames belched skyward.

Carl saw it at almost the same time Marc did. He grabbed the trooper by the arm and jerked him to his feet. Both Carl and the trooper scrambled for safety.

Marc didn't hesitate. He was up and running for the Leeco rig. Carl and the trooper were only steps behind him now. When they were twenty feet from the safety of the Leeco rig, the ground shook and vibrated. A roar of deafening thunder filled the air. Flames licked at the sky as thick towers of black smoke churned toward the clouds.

The concussion sent the trooper and both Highway Warriors to the ground. All three men instinctively covered their heads and ears with their arms. When the thunder stopped, the three men were up and scurrying for permanent cover.

Marc and Carl made it, but the trooper didn't. A second cataclysmic explosion rained fiery debris in every direction. A sailing piece of safety glass set in motion by the violent eruption caught the trooper in the top of the head and sent him reeling to the ground. Carl turned around and grabbed the trooper. He dragged his uncon-scious body to safety an instant before the third explo-sion rattled the earth around them.

The Highway Warriors breathlessly watched as flames licked upward in roaring towers a hundred feet in the air. Both highway patrol cars and the BMW burned out of control. An acrid odor filled the air from the burning raw gasoline that undermined all three vehicles and then consumed them.

The state trooper was bleeding badly, but at least he was still breathing. Carl improvised a compress with his handkerchief and applied it to the gaping head wound. The intense heat and the dense smoke made the air heavy and breathing uncomfortable.

"This guy needs medical help. He's hurt bad," Carl said excitedly, then gasped for breath.

Marc looked away from the flaming wreckage at Carl and the fallen trooper. "I can go make a call on the ComSat link or see if I can get a cellular frequency. I'll get the first-aid kit from the rig."

Carl didn't hesitate. "Go for it. I'll keep trying to slow the bleeding."

Marc jumped from the cover of the Leeco overroad rig. The instant he stood and started for the cab, he heard sirens wailing just beyond the line of traffic stalled behind them. "We got company. Might be in our best interest if we get the trooper to the side of the road and haul ass. There'll be a lot of questions when the other boys in blue get here."

"I'm for that. We don't need the questions and they certainly don't need the answers." Carl was already up and moving the injured state trooper to the shoulder of the road.

Marc glanced once more at the flaming, twisted wreckage that blocked the interstate highway. Beyond the cars lay two less dirtbags to squeeze the life's blood of innocents. "One thing I got to know," Marc said as the siren's intensity increased.

Carl was straining from the dead weight of the injured trooper as he tried to move him off the road.

Through clenched teeth, he answered Marc. "Yeah, what's that?"

"What those dirtbags were carrying in that attaché case that they were willing to die for."

"I got the trooper. Why don't you go find out before the troops get here."

Marc broke into a dead run, his head tucked down toward his chest to decrease the effects of the heat from the flaming wreckage. In seconds he reached the charred body of the shooter from the BMW. The singed leather attaché case was still in the dead man's grip. The fireball from the initial explosion had caused the exposed surface of the case to burn. The dead man's clothing smoked, and the odor of burning flesh together with the acrid smell from the flaming vehicles was nauseating. Marc felt his stomach churn as he leaned over and grabbed the smoking case from the shooter's death grip. He turned immediately and sprinted back to the Leeco rig.

The sirens were closer now as Marc stopped beside Carl and the injured trooper. Carl was kneeling beside the injured lawman and applying pressure to the gaping head wound in an attempt to slow the loss of blood. He looked up when Marc stopped beside him. "What's in the case?"

Marc dropped down beside Carl and laid the case on the gravel. He touched the locking hinge quickly to see if it was hot. It wasn't. He flipped the lock release but the case didn't open. In the next instant, he was out with his Buck pocket knife. He opened the blade and pryed at the lock hinge. It opened immediately. Marc lifted the top of the attaché case.

"Holy shit!" Carl's eyes widened. "Must be a couple of hundred thousand dollars worth there."

The sirens were very close now. And judging by the sound, the drivers of the emergency vehicles were threading their way through the stalled traffic. Marc scrutinized the contents of the case. There were two off-white bricks of what appeared to be uncut cocaine wrapped tightly in clear plastic. Beside the bricks there were at least three dozen small plastic bags filled with pebble-size white rocks—crack. "Yeah, must be. But it sure as hell ain't worth dyin' for."

"I second that," Carl agreed.

Marc slammed the lid closed. "Let's leave it with the trooper and get away from this place."

———

Glen Hawthorn watched the white lines stream past him as he rolled the eighteen-wheeler east on Interstate 40 outside of Oklahoma City. The prescription medication had quickly cleared his stuffy sinuses, and that made driving much easier. Now all he had to do was make up for the time the dock workers had cost him. He had a reputation for delivering his loads on time, and he'd be damned if he was going to let some smart-ass dock foreman change that.

Above the windshield of the Freightliner, the Escort radar detector monitored the highway ahead of him. He had the CB tuned to channel 19 listening for Smokie reports. He wasn't one to talk a lot on the little radio, but he always enjoyed listening. The conversation between other truckers kept him abreast of the police protection waiting farther down the highway.

Aside from having to make up for lost time, Hawthorn was relaxed. He let his mind drift away to Dallas. When he had talked to his wife yesterday by telephone, they had made plans for a large family cookout the day after he got home. He could smell the charcoal and the delectable aroma of a thick Texas steak sizzling on the grill. The very thought made him hungry. And the only thing that stood between him and the steak was one stop in Fort Smith and a couple of hours on the highway.

Hawthorn decided to take a short break at the truckstop in Fort Smith after his truck was unloaded at the freight yard. At the truckstop he could shower, enjoy a nourishing hot meal, fill the fuel tanks, and then make a straight run for Dallas. If his luck held out and the dock foreman in Fort Smith wasn't a jerk, then he could easily make it before midnight. That would allow time for a good night's rest before the cookout. And this was one break between highway runs that Glen Hawthorn was really looking forward to.

He pressed harder on the accelerator and took the rig to seventy miles per hour . . . five miles per hour over the speed limit. Time to make up that lost time.

Ronnie Hazelwood had grown to like Donald Puckett although he had known the man only an hour. But in that hour he had come to appreciate the way the guy thought. It had become increasingly difficult to find someone who didn't mind dipping into a stash of goods here and there in order to ease the pressure a little.

Hazelwood thought it ironic that the "in thing" was to publicly say no to drugs and then go snort a little coke. While the politicians screamed for better and more rigorous drug enforcement, they met on the weekends with their friends and snorted some blow. But the real "in thing" for the yuppie crowd was the ever increasing availability of designer drugs. The effects of some of the latest chemical developments ranged from mild to maddening. The beauty of it was, the mind-altering substances were the products of yuppie chemists who frequently sat in high corporate places. These chemists had found that their peers would pay dearly for special chemical mixtures that set the modern mind free of all worries. So, when Donald Puckett had initiated the conversation about designer drugs, Ronnie Hawthorn had listened attentively. Being a driver with a strong sense of adventure, he was always ready to try something new.

Hazelwood took his eyes off the road and looked at

Donald Puckett. "All right, man. You got a good source for some designer stuff, huh?"

David Foster grinned, exposing his teeth behind his beard. "The best. Good junk like this is hard to come by. My source is the best there is. Primo fine."

Hazelwood laughed and slapped the steering wheel. "I like it, man. I like it. When do I get a sample?"

"How far is the next rest area?"

"I don't know for sure. Let's see where we are. Yeah, there's a yardstick. Okay, ten miles, maybe twelve."

Foster nodded his head. "Very good. I'm tellin' you, you'll get a real rise out of this stuff."

"What did you say it's called?"

"Angel Fly or Forever Mellow, whichever you prefer. It'll take you places you've never been."

Hazelwood slapped the steering wheel again. "I love it, man. What's in the stuff?"

"Just a couple of natural ingredients. You find them just about anywhere. Primo extracts. It'll set you free."

"How did you find this shit, man?"

"My friend, the chemist. He gets his kicks creating compounds to take all the pain away."

"Hot damn! Can I still drive? I mean, you think it'll be safe?"

"As safe as driving with anything else you take."

Hazelwood bounced once in the air-shock seat and slapped the steering wheel one more time. "All right. I can't wait."

Foster offered an observation. "You sure beat the hell out of that steering wheel when you get excited."

"Ah, shit, Donald, it's a habit like slapping your hands together or something. Ain't no thing."

"Right. How long you been driving?"

"Five, almost six years. Why?"

"You worry about driving when you're stoned?"

"Me? No. I'm a better driver when I'm all mellowed out. Takes the pressure off when these damned crazy four-wheelers screw up the highway. You know what I mean?"

Foster tried to act confused. "Not exactly."

Hazelwood's face became suddenly serious. "Damned four-wheelers, man. They got no respect for trucks. They drive like they own the damned road, you know? Well, they'll speed up to pass you and then they'll cut right back in front of you and slow down. You have to slam on the brakes to keep from creamin' their asses. Bastards got no respect. They ain't smart enough to realize we can't stop eighty thousand pounds of freight on a dime. If it wasn't for dumb-shit four-wheelers and gung-ho speed cops, drivin' would be a piece a cake. You could knock off some miles and shuck away some big bucks. Time was when you could do that, but not anymore. I got me a new attitude. I say to hell with it and get high. I mean, who gives a shit?"

Foster acted concerned. "You ever have a wreck in one of these things?"

"Hell, yes. Well, a couple a fender-benders. Nothing big-time. Once I tagged a four-wheeler that cut me off, and another time some dipshit in a Toyota slammed on his brakes in a downpour and I had to lock it up to keep from running right over him. I jackknifed the rig and rolled over in the median. Dumb bastard that caused it kept right on his merry way. Probably never knew what he'd done. And you know what's the bitch?"

Foster raised his eyebrows when he looked at Hazelwood. "No, what?"

"I'm the one old Smoky gave the ticket for both of them wrecks. Pissed me off, too, cause I wasn't responsible for either one. I guess if I hadn't been poppin' some speed when I jackknifed the rig, I'd have run the Toyota driver down. The stuff made me a hell of a lot more alert 'cause I was on a long haul with a bunch of hours under the wheel. The speed kept me going, man."

Foster sensed Hazelwood's anger. "I guess you weren't hurt in either wreck, were you?"

"Naw, not really. I picked up a few bruises and a bloody nose in the jackknife. That's about it. Must have been luck."

"Tell me something, Ronnie. Why do you keep drivin' if there's so much you don't like?"

"Hey, don't get me wrong. I love what I do, man. I wouldn't want to do anything else unless I was rich and didn't have to work. The places I been and the things I've seen, shit, I wouldn't trade that for a million bucks. No way."

David Foster grinned. "That's the way I am. I love what I'm doing. Nobody to answer to, no schedules, no time clocks, no bullshit. I gave all that back to the people who want to be tied down by it. It's not for me anymore. I'm a free dude now."

"Where you from, anyway?"

Foster stared out the windshield for a long moment. He thought about the question before he answered. For some reason the question sent a barrage of visions sailing though his mind. He knew he had to choose his words carefully and answer the driver but not tell all he knew. "Ohio, but that was a long time ago."

"The Buckeye State. They got unmerciful, badass speed cops up there. Almost as bad as the Communist State, but not quite."

Foster didn't understand. "The Communist State?"

Hazelwood laughed. "That's trucker's talk for Virginia. Talk about a bad bunch of assholes. Well, Virginia's got 'em. They even got dogs that'll search your truck at the weigh stations if they think you got drugs on board. I think some of them Virginia troopers would arrest their own grandmothers if they caught 'em with a joint. They got no mercy. Period."

Foster suddenly found renewed interest. "You ever been searched by the dogs?"

"No, not me. I got a buddy that was once. They nailed him at the scales 'cause he was a little overloaded. They checked him out and the trooper told him he thought he was on drugs. They arrested him and sent the dogs into his cab. They got a nickel bag of pot, but that damned dog ripped the interior of that cab to shreds. Took out all the upholstery and made the sleeper look like a couple of wildcats had been tryin' to screw each other in it. I saw the rig a little later and they had totalled it. I don't think that's right. Man ought to be able to do what he wants just like me and you. What do you think?" Hazelwood's face had taken on a hard, mean look.

David Foster smiled inside, but on the outside he held a look of deep concern. "Sounds hard to me. That's rough."

Hazelwood still looked mean. "Yeah, it's rough all right. They fined my friend ten thousand dollars and gave him a year in the joint. Poor bastard lost his business, his rig, and his wife over one little ole nickel bag."

Foster had another barrage of thoughts crashing through his mind. He agreed with Hazelwood—it wasn't right. The punishment was too damned lenient. Foster thought Hazelwood's friend was lucky he had gotten caught by the police instead of the hitchhiker. Because when the police caught a truck-driving druggie, the perpetrator would eventually get out of jail. When the hitchhiker caught one . . . well. "Sorry to hear about your friend. Hope things got better for him."

Hazelwood stared hard at the road in front of him. He hesitated for a moment, then answered. "Yeah, well, eventually it got better. Poor bastard had to move to the other side of the country and change his name. He finally got another truck-driving job with a produce company out of Fresno. Screwed his life up big-time. Oh, well. The moral is never get your ass caught. Right?"

"Right."

"Okay, the rest area is a mile ahead. You gotta take a leak?"

"I could handle it."

"Good, we'll hit the john and then get us a soda pop from the vending machines. I want to try some of your designer shit."

Foster laughed. "I'm tellin' you, Ronnie, it'll do things for you you've never had done. Satisfaction guaranteed. You'll feel things you never knew existed, and it doesn't take long to set you free."

Hazelwood moved the big overroad rig into the slow lane of Interstate 40 and got off at the rest area. He and Foster went to the rest room. Foster was careful to stay slightly behind Hazelwood so no one would really notice they were together. Once they finished in the men's room, they met by the vending machines beside the building.

Hazelwood popped quarters into the slot and pressed the buttons for the drinks. "Drinks are on me."

"That's not really necessary. I can handle it."

Hazelwood chuckled. "Hey, my man, it's the least I can do."

Both men returned to the rig and climbed aboard.

Hazelwood was anxious. "I'm ready to get mellow."

Foster opened his backpack and removed a small bundle of aluminum foil. He unwrapped it and took two tablets the size of a large vitamin C tablet. He examined them closely and handed one to Hazelwood. "Enjoy."

Hazelwood took the tablet, looked it over carefully, and plopped it into his mouth. "Looks like vitamins." He washed the tablet down with his drink and sat back in his seat with a smile of anticipation across his face.

Foster followed Hazelwood's lead. He plopped his placebo into his mouth and washed it down. He waited for the satisfying effect—on Hazelwood.

Suddenly, Hazelwood was trembling and then the trembles became violent convulsions. He was shaking and his fingers curled inward toward his palms. His eyes were bulging. The texture of his skin became clammy, with a bluish tint that soon turned to purple. He struggled for breath as he shook in the driver's seat. He tried to get words out, but his vocal cords wouldn't work. He was gasping and shaking like a man on the verge of death. "Jesus Christ . . . what's in these things? Oh, I'm dying."

Foster was cool and unmoved as he watched the drug-loving trucker struggle vainly. He gripped the door handle and gathered his backpack. His face was vacant, deathlike. Foster pulled a dried rose from a small pouch in his backpack and placed it on the instrument console. "I told you, natural ingredients. Concentrated resins from Fly Amanita, Death Cup, and Angel of Death mushrooms . . . all on a vitamin C tablet. You have about another thirty seconds before the Fly Amanita toxins cause your nervous system to shut down, and then your heart will stop. You really shouldn't drive a truck and do drugs. Only a dumb son of a bitch would do that. Remember what you said, don't get caught. You lose. Good-bye, druggie."

Chapter Five

They were too late. Marc and Carl turned away from the injured trooper just in time to see the first of the emergency vehicles arrive behind the Leeco overroad rig. Another state trooper jumped from the car and ran in the direction of the Highway Warriors.

The trooper was not only excited, he was nervous. "What the hell happened here?"

Marc looked at Carl, then at the trooper. "We're not real sure. We just got here a minute or two ago ourselves. This officer was injured and we tried to help him. There's another one over behind those burning cars, but I don't think he made it. Looks like a drug bust went sour or something. We found this man lying on the ground injured, so we treated him. He had that case of stuff there that looks like drugs or something."

The trooper scanned over the situation and knelt beside the injured trooper on the ground. "I'll check on the ETA of the ambulance. "I don't think he's hurt too badly. You guys see any of this?"

Carl answered. "No, sir, not really. We just saw the man on the ground and tried to help." Carl hoped the lies worked, and he was thankful that he and Marc had put the Uzis back into the Leeco rig before the trooper arrived on the scene.

The trooper ran back to his car and returned a minute or two later. "Ambulance should be here in another minute or two. How is it, with all this traffic backed up, that you guys are the first vehicle in the line and you didn't see anything?"

Marc shrugged his shoulders. "I guess there just wasn't much traffic. Things were pretty much like you see them when we got here. Now we did move the injured trooper from over by the burning cars. He's the only one that had a pulse. The way things were burning a few minutes ago, looked like he might burn to death if we didn't get him away from there."

The trooper wasn't sure whether to buy the trucker's story or hold them for questioning. The facts almost spoke for themselves, which made it more difficult to make a decision. The fact was, there was an attaché case with what appeared to be a lot of drugs in it and an injured state trooper who had been treated for his wounds. He decided that if the two big men were lying, they certainly had every opportunity to leave before anyone else arrived on the scene. And if they weren't telling the truth, then they could have disappeared with the drugs. But they hadn't, for whatever reason, chosen to do that. They were here and they were calm. "A lot of people will be very happy to hear what you guys did for this injured lawman. I think you truckers get a bad rap sometimes. Nobody ever shouts very loudly about the good things you guys do. You've probably saved this man's life. That was a very heroic thing to do."

Marc nodded. "Nothing heroic about it. They had the road blocked and there wasn't much choice but to stop. We did for this man what we would have done for anybody else in the same situation."

The trooper smiled. "You're modest. Don't be."

Carl looked the man in the eyes. "Look, if it's all the same to you, we'd like to be on our way. We've been here long enough and we have a schedule to keep in Dallas. Would it be all right if we leave?"

The trooper hesitated. "I'd like to get your names and your company's name just in case there are any questions that come up unanswered. And I'm sure the man whose life you saved might want to give you a call of thanks when he recovers. Other than that, I don't see any reason why you can't be on your way. But tell me truthfully, did you see anything happen here?"

"Nothing," Marc replied without hesitation. "We just happened on it. Fate does that sometimes. It puts you in places you'd rather not be. My name is Marc Lee and that's my partner, Carl Browne. We run for Leeco Freight Lines out of Dallas."

The state trooper wrote all of the information in a small pocket notebook. "You got a phone number where you can be reached in Dallas?"

Marc gave him the number of the Leeco terminal.

The trooper finished his notes and looked sternly at the two Highway Warriors. "Okay, I guess there isn't much else I can do. You men can get on your way. Thanks for what you did. For your records or your information, I'm Trooper R. L. Jones. We'll be in touch with you if there's anything else we need to talk to you about."

The ambulance approached by running mostly on the shoulder of the road to get around the stalled interstate traffic. Paramedics were out of the vehicle before it was even completely stopped. They rushed to the fallen trooper and initiated emergency medical treatment.

Marc and Carl watched until the injured lawman was loaded into the back of the ambulance. The state trooper watched every movement. Finally he closed the top on the charred attaché case and removed it to the trunk of his patrol car. When the Highway Warriors were satisfied that the contraband was in safe hands, they returned to the cab of the customized Leeco rig and climbed aboard.

One of the paramedics stayed with the injured lawman while the other left to examine the first fallen lawman behind the burned cars. He covered the dead man with a sheet and then examined the two men from the BMW.

Marc dropped the rig into gear and moved slowly to

the left shoulder of the road. Once the rig had cleared the latest killing ground, he changed gears and accelerated.

Carl broke the silence. "You know we haven't heard the last of that one, don't you?"

"Probably. It all depends on what the autopsy shows on the dirtbags and what that injured cop can remember. I'm hoping the head wound will help him forget certain things, if you catch my drift."

Carl wasn't easily convinced. "Could we be so lucky?"

Marc brought the rig up to highway cruising speed and settled back in his air-shock seat. "Let's hope. We handled it the only way we could. We couldn't walk off and leave an unconscious lawman with a case full of cocaine and crack lying beside him. Sure as we did that, some other scumbag would have come along and taken it. Guess who they'd be looking for then?"

Carl relaxed in his seat also. "You're right. One of the risks of the profession, I suppose. That mess sure got touchy for a minute. I thought the trooper was gonna lock our asses up."

"He was scared, that's all. Everything went down pretty fast back there. I guess we know now why the asshole driving the BMW wouldn't stop. If I'd been hauling that much dope, I wouldn't have stopped either."

Carl flexed his arms and looked at the highway ahead. "Look at it this way, that's two more zits off the ass of society. And this time, the taxpayers won't have to feed them for thirty years."

Marc expressed concern. "Maybe we should have checked them a little closer. Those assholes had to be working for somebody unless they were freelancers. Either way, it might be interesting to find out where they got that coke."

Carl nodded. "Yeah, and I'll tell you something else I'd like to know more about, those truckers that have been found dead. You know, the ones in the news article."

Marc didn't answer for a long moment. "Well, we have the technology. Give Brittin a call and put him to work. He's probably sitting behind a nice desk in an air-conditioned office and bitching because he has nothing to do."

Carl reached for the microphone attached to the remote-control head of the Icom IC-V100 VHF transceiver mounted on the high-tech instrument console. He pressed the microphone button to key the transmitter. "Barnburner, this is Pathfinder. Do you read me? Over."

In little more than a heartbeat, the electronic communications system locked in to the uplink frequency of ComSat-D. The ComSat satellite orbited the earth in an elliptical orbit twenty-five thousand miles out in space. The system linked together anywhere in the country and formed the backbone of the Defense Department's nationwide radio repeater system. The top-secret communications project gave its users point-to-point contact from almost anywhere in the United States and some foreign countries. Users of ComSat-D system could access and effectively communicate from virtually any point in the United States by using a low-power handheld transceiver. A beautiful feature of the system was the digital encoding and decoding circuitry that changed code cypher and frequency sixty times each second, making unauthorized access or monitoring of the frequencies virtually impossible without a mutual electronic subtone "handshake."

There was no immediate answer. Carl pressed the transmit button again. "Pathfinder to Barnburner. Do you read me? Over."

A familiar voice crackled through the Icom's speaker—Brittin Crain in Washington, D.C. The Dallas cop turned FBI liaison for the Highway Warriors had been a longtime friend of Marc Lee's before the war on crime started. "Roger, Pathfinder. This is Barnburner. Go ahead with your traffic."

Carl made his request and waited for Crain's reply.

Fifteen minutes passed before the Icom finally crackled with the familiar Texas drawl. "Pathfinder, this is Barnburner. Sorry for the delay, guys. We have gathered the information you requested. You may be on to something. Since different law enforcement agencies were involved in each case, there has been little exchange of information. We assimilated all of the police reports from the various agencies on all three cases. Aside from peculiar causes of death, there is one very interesting link. In all three cases, there was a dried flower left with the body. I think maybe the killer is trying to deliver some kind of message. Drugs were found either on the body or in the vehicle, and each time the flower was a rose."

———

David Foster had stayed until he was sure Ronnie Hazelwood was dead. The final seconds had been torturous for the renegade drug-using truck driver. Hazelwood had bent over double from the ghastly abdominal pain, and he tried to scream. The scream finally succumbed to a futile plea for mercy . . . for his life. Foster had watched the scenario through vacant eyes that now knew no mercy. When the Fly Amanita toxins finally seized control of Hazelwood's nervous system and brutally stopped his heart, Foster's blank facial expression yielded to a smile of satisfaction.

Foster carefully examined the rest area for wandering eyes. He moved Hazelwood's body into the area between the seats and climbed into the driver's seat. With the driver's door facing the interstate highway, no one would be able to see him leave the death cab. And besides, there was very little activity in the rest area at the moment. That made timing perfect for escape from the scene of his lethal retribution.

Assured that no one was looking his way, Foster climbed from the cab and stopped on the running board. He leaned back inside, took a rag from under the driver's seat, and wiped everything clean that he had touched inside. He reached over to the instrument console and picked up the dried rose. In what was almost a ceremonial ritual, he placed it gently on the dead truck driver's body. Another smile split across his bearded face as he jumped to the ground. A firm push, using only his knuckles, closed the rig's door. David Foster walked to the entry ramp onto Interstate 40. He waited for an approaching eighteen-wheeler and threw his thumb high into the air, but the driver didn't stop.

Foster started walking along the shoulder of the road. He walked for more than a mile, hoisting his thumb high each time an eighteen-wheeler approached behind him on the super highway. For the average man, it might have seemed that destiny wanted him to walk—but not David Foster. He knew some lonely driver would stop and offer him a ride at any minute. And if he was lucky, it might be another druggie.

He heard the vehicle slowing behind him. Foster glanced over his shoulder to take a look. This time, it wasn't an eighteen-wheeler. The approaching vehicle was a cop car.

Foster took a deep breath and spoke to himself. *Be calm, David. He doesn't know anything. Be calm just like the thousands of rehearsals.*

The officer stopped not more than ten feet behind Foster. The light bar atop the patrol car came to life with rotating blue lights, and then the officer stepped out. He approached Foster carefully. "How are you?"

Foster was cool. "Fine, Officer."

The officer stopped walking three or four feet from Foster. "Would you mind stepping over to the side of my vehicle please?"

Foster tried to put on his best stunned face. "Is there some problem, Officer?"

"No, I'd just like to talk with you a moment."

David Foster walked back to the side of the patrol car like the officer had requested. "Am I doing something wrong?"

"No, only a precaution. Do you have some kind of identification?"

Foster hesitated and watched every move the officer made, knowing full well the officer was also scrutinizing his every move. "Uh, I have a Social Security card and an old draft card. Will that do?"

The officer nodded his head. "May I see them, please?"

Foster reached into his right rear pocket and found a faded, folded nylon camouflage wallet. He fumbled through it for the ID. "Sure, here you are." He handed it to the officer.

The officer accepted the cards and looked at them carefully. "How long have you been walking, Mr. Puckett?"

"You mean today?"

"Yes."

"I started out a little after sunup this morning. I don't have a watch, so I don't know what time it is now. I caught one ride with a couple of fellows in a blue station wagon, but they got off at the last exit. It's been shoe leather since then."

"Where are you headed, Mr. Puckett."

"I guess Fort Smith or somewhere near there for the night. After that, back on the road until I get to Albuquerque."

The officer pursued the lead. "Are you a resident of Albuquerque, Mr. Puckett?"

Foster smiled. "No, I have some friends there. Thought I might spend a little time with them, and then, well, who knows where after that. Have I done something wrong?"

The officer looked hard at the draft card. "Is this name, Donald J. Puckett, correct?"

"Yes, sir."

The officer found a potential way to trip the guy up. "And the DOB, October fourth, nineteen fifty-six. Is that correct also?"

"No, it's nineteen fifty-eight."

The officer glanced back down at the card for a simulated second look, but he already knew Donald Puckett was correct, and maybe that meant the guy was straight. "Would you mind waiting beside my car for a moment while I attend to some radio traffic?"

"You mean while you run me through NCIC to see if I have any outstanding warrants? You're wasting your time, but sure, I'll wait. I'll tell you now, I'm clean."

Foster's comment caught the officer off guard. "You're very bright. You must have been checked before."

"Once or twice. I also have a master's degree in criminal justice. You might say I'm out here on the road on a field trip. A little hands-on research." He hoped the lie worked.

"I see. I suppose in that case, you know that this is a fundamental procedure and it'll only take a minute." The officer walked back to the front of his car and then to the driver's door. He got inside and picked up his radio microphone.

Foster watched while the officer made his radio call. Now he wasn't nervous at all because he had done a sufficient amount of homework to know that Donald J. Puckett with that Social Security number and date of birth was squeaky clean. He could hardly be otherwise. The real Donald J. Puckett from northern Arkansas had died in 1962 when he was four years old.

It took three or four minutes, but the officer finally came back to where Foster was standing. "Okay, Mr. Puckett. You check out. For your safety, we like to know who we have passing through this part of the country. I hope I haven't inconvenienced you too much. I'm going in the direction of Fort Smith. Would you like a ride?"

Foster took his ID cards back when the officer offered them. "Thanks, but I think I'll stay out here on the road and enjoy the fresh air. I appreciate the offer and I understand you're only doing your job. I admire that, because I'm out here doing mine."

The officer was puzzled by Foster's remark, but he let it drop. "Okay, it's your choice. Listen, be careful who you hitch a ride with out here on the highway. There are a lot of strange and sometimes not-so-nice people rolling along these concrete thoroughfares. I wouldn't want to find you in a ditch somewhere."

Foster smiled. "I appreciate your concern. I'll take proper precautions."

"Have a nice day, Mr. Puckett, and I hope you find whatever it is you're looking for out here."

Foster nodded his head. "I will, Officer. Eventually, I will."

———

Willie Barnes spotted the hitchhiker the instant his big rig topped the rise. Halfway down the hill, the bearded backpacker stood with his thumb held high. Barnes hesitated and questioned his own judgment. Then he decided to stop. His mind had immediately raced back to the late sixties and early seventies when he himself had been a bearded flower child. And he remembered the long nights beside the highway beneath a tattered blanket and a canopy of stars for his one-night home. In the instant before he stepped on the Peterbilt's brakes, his mind had retrieved fond recollections of those carefree days filled with women, avoiding the draft, and scoring the next hit of acid. And in the instant of that memory, he felt a broad smile crease his face.

Barnes moved the overroad rig into the right lane and then into the emergency-stopping lane. He let the big rig roll gently to a stop slightly ahead of the hitchhiker. When he looked in the mirror, the guy with the beard was running along the shoulder of the road and then beside the long Dorsey trailer. In the next instant the bearded face peeped through the cab's passenger window. When the door opened, Willie spoke with a grin. "You goin' my way?"

David Foster answered quickly. "It looks like I am. I could sure use the ride."

"Well, hop in. I'm only going as far as Fort Smith. If that'll help, you're welcome to come aboard. I could use the company."

The hitchhiker nodded in agreement. He removed his backpack and held it across his waist as he climbed in. He allowed his hand to slip into one of the compartments that held his big survival knife. His hand wrapped around the handle of the big blade and David Foster was ready. "Boy, that sure sounds good to me. I was beginning to think I was gonna have to stay out here through the night."

Barnes laughed. "I been there. It's been twenty years or more, but I been there. Where you headed?"

Foster shot back, his hand still concealed inside the pack. "Fort Smith sounds good to me."

Barnes said, "Man, oh, man, I remember those days. Back in my day, we called guys like you hippies or flower children. Hell, I was one myself. I've been a little out of touch with the culture. What's the in-word now days?"

Foster managed a laugh while he decided whether or not he was going to kill the trucker. "Crazy."

Barnes moved the rig forward and signaled his intention to get back on the highway. As the rig accelerated he spoke. "Well, I guess now all of us hippies have been upgraded to yuppies. Guess some of us never came out of it, though. I'm one of 'em. Quit hitchhiking and got a good job driving. I figured what the hell, I can do the same things I did twenty years ago like travel and see new places, only now I get paid for it. I also got away from all those crazy drugs we used to play around with. I learned early on that all that shit ain't good for you.

Drugs and drivin' don't mix. Well, now that I've told you my life story, what's yours?"

Foster settled into the passenger's seat. He loosened his grip on the knife inside his backpack. He let his hand slide free, and the pack slipped to the floor of the Peterbilt. If this one didn't like drugs, he decided to let him live . . . for now. "Not much different than yours really. I just got sick of it all and decided to take a little sabbatical. You might say I'm taking inventory of America. I guess you could say I'm a modern-day flower child with a purpose."

Chapter Six

Glen Hawthorn splashed more of the soothing cold water on his face. He wasn't sure why, but the cool water relieved the pain from his stuffy sinuses. He reached for a paper towel beside the sink and dried his face and hands. That accomplished, he reached into his travel bag and found the prescription bottle for the sinus medication. Hawthorn twisted the top off and let two capsules drop into his hand. He plopped them into his mouth and got a handful of water from the sink to wash them down. One more paper towel to dry his face and hands and he would head out of the truckstop for the road.

Hawthorn tossed the soiled paper towel into the trash can. That's when he noticed the man watching him. The guy was bearded, a backpack at his feet, and he was washing his hands at the sink beside the one Hawthorn had just left. Hawthorn zipped his travel bag and moved toward the door.

The bearded man at the sink looked up as he dried his own face. "Excuse me, driver. Which way you headed?"

Glen Hawthorn stopped. He didn't usually like to talk to strangers, especially ones that looked like hitchhikers. "Uh, Dallas. Why?"

"Amazing, I'm trying to get a ride there. Could I interest you in a rider?"

Hawthorn hesitated. "I don't normally do that, but I'm empty so I guess there's no harm. I'm leaving just as soon as I buy some cigarettes. You ready?"

David Foster grinned. "Sure, as soon as I dry off. That won't take but a minute."

"Okay, I'll get my cigarettes and meet you out in the lobby by the pay phones."

"Okay. Thanks."

Foster felt a rush of adrenaline. He had scored another one. Another drugged out truck driver who shouldn't be on the highway to kill innocent people. But in what was due the bastard, this one wouldn't be on the highway much longer. David Foster made up his mind to that. He finished wiping his face, gathered his backpack, and left the restroom.

As David Foster walked from the rest room into the lobby of the big truckstop, he thought about the driver who had given him a ride to Fort Smith. Foster thought the guy was okay. He had spent his time messing with substances that altered his mental state, but he had awakened before it was too late. And now that driver was one who took his work seriously and enjoyed it. In doing that, he didn't find the need to rely on chemical substances to keep him going. During their short time together, Foster had even found that Willie Barnes was very much against drugs now. Barnes had brought him to the truckstop and let him out. They had parted as friends, and David Foster knew he would probably never see the big guy again.

What was important now was to see that another driver with reflexes, judgment, and vision impaired by chemicals was not allowed to travel the same highway as innocent motorists. If, by eliminating thoughtless bastards from society, Foster could save just one more innocent life, then his mission was a success. His vendetta had achieved its purpose. Only one demon remained untamed. And that, too, would come with time.

Foster saw the driver step away from the cashier and tuck the cigarettes into his shirt pocket. He dropped in step beside the man. "I don't think I introduced myself. I'm Don Puckett."

The driver didn't break his stride as he continued to walk toward the exit doors leading into the truck parking area behind the truckstop. "Pleased to make your acquaintance. I'm Glen Hawthorn."

Foster forced a smile. "I really appreciate the ride. Thumbin' isn't quite as easy as it used to be."

Hawthorn pushed the doors open and they walked into the parking lot. Eighteen-wheelers were parked in every available space. "Yeah, well, I'll tell you what. I don't usually pick up riders, but I'm headed back to Dallas for a week or ten days of no white lines and no speed cops. I'm gonna pop the top on a cold one and prop my feet up by the pool when I get this rig checked in at the terminal. I sure am ready for a break. Guess what that means is, you got lucky. You caught me at a good time."

Foster was quick to reply. "I can stand a little luck."

They reached Glen Hawthorn's rig. He unlocked the cab and climbed inside. Then he leaned over to the passenger's door and unlocked it. David Foster opened the door and threw his backpack inside. He climbed in and made himself comfortable in the passenger's seat.

Hawthorn fired the big diesel and let it warm for a moment. "I probably won't stop until I get to I-Thirty at Texarkana. Not much to do on U.S. Seventy-one South. There's a truckstop there at Thirty, and we'll get one more cup of hot-C before I make the final leg into Dallas. That a problem for you?"

Foster rummaged through his backpack as if he were looking for something. "Not at all. I'm the beggar, remember?"

"Maybe I'm bein' a tad bit nosey, but what you got goin' in Dallas? Relatives?"

"No, some friends I haven't seen in a few years. Thought I might stop in for a few days before I head out again."

Hawthorn had the rig in motion. He threaded his way out of the maze of parked overroad rigs until he reached the highway. "I sure will be glad to get to Dallas. I rolled in here a while ago with a load from OK City. Got her off-loaded and came by the truckstop for a cup and to freshen up a little. Now it's dead-head to the big D and some welcomed R and R. Probably shouldn't have had but one cup. This truck stop coffee goes through me like flour through a sifter. I said I wasn't gonna stop until Texarkana, but I'll probably have to make a quick one and take a leak."

Foster let most of the commentary fly past. "Coffee does that to some people."

"Right, and I'm one of 'em. What do you do for a livin'?"

Foster hesitated, unsure of whether or not to be honest with the trucker. He decided it wouldn't matter one way or the other in an hour or two. "Believe it or not, I used to be a businessman. I got fed up with the hustle and bustle and said to hell with it. I'm taking a break from it all to see America."

Hawthorn shifted gears and changed lanes on the highway. "Must be nice. Me, I'm too tied down to the mortgage and car payments to be able to do that. I gotta keep these eighteen-wheels rollin' if I'm gonna keep my ship afloat."

Foster felt the memories crashing unexpectedly around him like bolts of lightning from a cloudy sky. Mortgage. Car payments. Family. Now he had none of that. And why? Some bastard taking drugs and driving an eighteen-wheeler like a maniac had taken it from him. An inconsiderate, selfish son of a bitch who gave no thought to the repercussions of his own actions and thought of nothing but his own gratification. He had encroached the line of human rights and extracted the only thing that mattered from David Foster's life. And now here he sat, in the front seat of another eighteen-wheeler with another asshole who couldn't make it through the day without the assistance of chemical compounds. The guy hadn't told him that, but he knew it. He had seen it in the rest room. Pills or capsules or something from a brown bottle . . . and the bastard took them and went straight to the cab of his rig and then started driving. It had to stop.

Foster had silently worked himself into a rage. His blood pressure was sailing through the roof. He reached into the backpack and came out with his Ruger Mark II .22 pistol. He shoved it toward Glen Hawthorn. "Find a place to stop this truck. Do it carefully. I get real nervous when I ride in these things."

Hawthorn took his eyes off the road and glanced over at the man he knew as Don Puckett. He couldn't believe what he saw and he was scared. "What? Are you crazy? What is this?"

Foster's voice was cold, his face expressionless. But inside him the rage consumed his soul. "This is the end of the run for you, bastard. You've reached the terminal and it's for good this time."

Hawthorn kept the rig rolling. He wasn't sure which was running faster, the overroad rig or his heart. "I don't understand. What have I done to you?"

Foster laughed in Hawthorn's face. "It's your kind. You're the filth that smothers innocent lives. You and the ones just like you."

Hawthorn was talking fast. "Man, are you nuts? I ain't done nothin' to you. Hell, boy, I've never seen you before in my life. Why are you doin' this?"

Foster's face went cold again. "Nice try, asshole. It won't work. All of you druggies drivin' trucks and killin' innocent people. You gotta pay."

Hawthorn shook his head like he didn't believe what he was hearing. "Have you flipped out? I don't know what you're talkin' about."

Foster was feeling more anger now. The Ruger was extended in his right hand, rock steady even in the rage.

He spoke hard between tightly clenched teeth. "Stop this truck and do it now!"

Hawthorn didn't know what to do, so he laughed. "No way. You shoot me now and you're dead too. This rig is running sixty miles an hour. It'll make a hell of a crash without a driver. You ain't too likely to walk away from it. Go ahead, shoot me."

David Foster was cool, but he was losing his patience. He reached for the key switch with his left hand to shut the rig down. Hawthorn grabbed his arm and twisted, jerking Foster forward toward him. Foster struggled to get his arm free. He yelled. "I'll kill you. Let go now!"

Hawthorn twisted harder. "So do it and stop talkin' about it."

The rig was rolling erratically now, weaving across the center line and running from shoulder to shoulder on the blacktop. Cars ahead of the rig swerved to get out of the way. Hawthorn mashed the accelerator to gain more speed. He struggled with Foster's wrist with his right hand and steered the big overroad rig with his left. Behind the cab, the trailer moaned from the sharp, unexpected turns. The rig was almost out of control now, and Foster continued to wave the pistol in his right hand, but Hawthorn wasn't about to stop.

Foster shifted his weight in the seat and took a swing at Hawthorn's face with the barrel of the Ruger.

Hawthorn jerked his neck back and the swing missed.

The rig made a sharp turn and oscillated like a snake on hot sand. Hawthorn couldn't control it; Foster couldn't get his arm free.

Glen Hawthorn glanced at the speedometer—seventy-five miles per hour. He screamed at Don Puckett. "Give it up. Let the gun fall and maybe we won't die."

"Never!" Foster squeezed the Ruger's trigger and a

single shot smothered the stress-generated cries of the screaming face.

"It makes sense. I think we have a psychopathic serial killer on the loose." Marc glanced at Carl beside him in the Leeco cab and waited for a reaction.

Carl contemplated his response. He rubbed his chin and stared out the windshield while the rig rolled down the highway toward Dallas. "It's certainly far beyond coincidence. Question is, why truckers? Why has this person got a hard-on for eighteen-wheelers?"

"It could sure make for some interesting work. But unless Brittin can turn something through the Bureau, it'll be like looking for a pea on the bottom of a pond. Could be anybody from anywhere. And the reasons, well, the possibilities are endless."

Carl stared vacantly out the window, thinking more than actually looking. "If that's what we're dealing with, this person could hit again at any time. Maybe he already has and we just don't know it. It's a frightening thought . . . a random killer taking out truckers. God knows he has a plentiful supply of targets."

Marc steered the big Leeco rig over the blacktop as the broken white lines passed in a steady stream that resembled dots rather than lines. "The rose. What is the significance of the rose?"

"Trademark. Whoever this person is, he wants to be sure he gets credit for his work."

"At this point, there seems to be no reason for the Bureau to get involved. Unless Brittin can find a viola-tion of federal law, the Bureau has no interest. That's one of the major pitfalls of bureaucratic red tape. The three local law enforcement agencies involved with these killings may not even know there is a link."

"I thought that was one of the things the National Criminal Information Center was supposed to help clear up with their national computer system. What happened there?"

Marc smiled. "It works pretty well. For some things, at least. NCIC can record outstanding warrants, stolen property, escapees, driver's license info, title info . . . that sort of thing. As far as linking or finding a common ground for various crimes, the system falls short. According to Brittin, many of the police agencies that have access to the system aren't truly proficient with its operation. They learn to use certain portions of its functions and forget about the rest because they're too complicated to access. It's a dynamic system if it were ever fully utilized. Sure could put a dent in criminal activity if the system ever reached its full potential."

Carl glanced over his shoulder at Marc. "Why isn't it utilized?"

"Beats me. I suppose the system has fallen victim to tight budgets, low pay for operators, and too little time for proper training. It's a shame too. Here is a multimillion dollar system running at less than twenty-five percent of its capability. If the people in the Defense Department had waited for all the politicians to play their games, our nationwide repeater system and ComSat-D would never have been more than a dream. Once someone is willing to put his balls on the line and act, rather than wait, it's amazing what can be accomplished. Just like we did with ComSat. But you get the political boys involved and you can kiss it good-bye. Maybe that's what happened to NCIC."

Carl shrugged his shoulders. "When it comes to combating the criminal scum, I suppose that's one place a Big Brother computer system might be worth its salt as long as there were restraints."

Marc smiled. "Politicians again. Get them involved and what was designed for one purpose ends up in service for something else that is less than beneficial to society in general. Society, businesses specifically, are more concerned with exchanging credit card information than they are with detecting fleeing felons. It's the power of politics and the almighty dollar at work. Make a buck any way you can and if somebody is stealing part of it, let the honest people pick up the slack or write it off to the cost of doing business. The working man always pays for it one way or the other."

Carl didn't reply for a long moment. Then when he started to say something, a voice crackled across the Icom speaker.

"Pathfinder, this is Barnburner. Do you copy?"

Carl reached for the microphone and answered. "Go ahead, Barnburner. This is Pathfinder."

Brittin Crain's deep voice came across the speaker with a distinct Texas drawl. "Roger, Carl. Got something in the works that might put a link together for you. We have contacted the law enforcement agencies involved in all three slayings. I have all physical evidence from each of the crime scenes headed to airports to be flown into the FBI lab for analysis. Fortunately, each agency retained the rose found at the scene. Once the lab boys work their magic, we'll see if we have something concrete. Could be we have us a new kind of flower child for the nineteen-nineties. In the sixties, it was peace and love. In the nineties, looks like it's murder."

———

The rig was completely out of control. David Foster found himself slammed violently from one side of the passenger's seat to the other as the huge eighteen-wheeler rocked, shook, and oscillated back and forth across the highway. The shot had missed and the violent thrusts of the rig had caused the Ruger to sail from Foster's hands to some unknown place inside the cab.

Glen Hawthorn was fighting the steering wheel to maintain control of the runaway rig. A fleeting thought ran through his mind: he couldn't remember a time in his life when he had been more afraid. The rig was out of ~ontrol at seventy-five miles per hour and a crazy man with a gun was trying to kill him. But he realized there was no time for fear. He had to get control of the speeding overroad rig or both he and the gunman would certainly die. The fact that he was running deadhead to Dallas made the possibility of survival a little more likely. But still, the rig wasn't like a car. With a trailer attached to the fifth-wheel, the likelihood of a jackknife was ever present. And at the speed the eighteen-wheeler was running, a jackknife meant certain disaster. Hawthorn took his eyes off the road for a microinstant and glanced at the hitchhiker. And that's when he saw the man lunging for him. Hawthorn took his right hand off the steering wheel and threw a wild backhand punch at Puckett's face.

The punch missed, but when Puckett ducked backward Hawthorn could see that the gun was gone from his hand. Hawthorn looked at the highway and jerked his hand back to the steering wheel. What he saw caused panic to race through his body. Ahead of the rig now, a car was stalled in the right lane and the highway took a hard left turn. Glen Hawthorn knew it was over—one way or another.

In the passenger's seat, David Foster was dazed. His head had slammed into the window, and for a few seconds he saw little white lights twirling around in circles. He shook his head and shrugged his shoulders trying to get control of himself. Foster looked around the cab, frantically searching for the lost Ruger pistol. He saw it—on the floor between the seats. Foster made a mad dive for the gun and his hand wrapped around the grip. He moved the weapon upward, but a crashing hammer-fist landed a punishing blow to the top of his head. More little twinkling white lights appeared, and his vision blurred. His grip loosened on the Ruger and he felt it slipping from his fingers. Then Foster realized what was happening, and he regained his grasp around the pistol's grip. Hawthorn's hand kept hammering, striking, at his head. Foster jerked free of the onslaught, the Ruger shaking in his trembling right hand. He aimed the pistol toward Hawthorn's face and squeezed the trigger.

The shot resonated throughout the cab at the same instant the speeding overroad rig left the highway. The first impact with the elevated shoulder of the roadway sent Hawthorn and Foster sailing into the top of the cab. Both men landed back in their seats, and Foster could see Hawthorn's body go limp. David Foster looked out the windshield and saw a grove of large trees that the rig was headed straight for. He braced himself, the rig slowing little as it plowed through the field beside the highway. In that instant, David Foster knew he was going to die and he knew what his family must have felt in the microseconds before death darkened their vision. He held tightly to the instrument console and the lip of the seat. Then he closed his eyes and waited for the inevitable—death.

Suddenly, Foster felt himself tumbling inside the cab. Strange as it was, it reminded him of a jogging shoe inside a clothes dryer. There were loud metallic screams when the metal of the trailer collided with the ground. The harsh grinding sound of metal meeting metal filled the cab when the trailer finally jackknifed on its side and then tumbled totally out of control. The rig rolled over and over and over. Clouds of dirt and dust went airborne in the wake of the dying overroad machine. The diesel engine spit, coughed, and then died from the unnatural traumatic impact. When it finally stopped, the massive eighteen-wheeler had been reduced to a pile of twisted and tangled metal resting on its side against the earth like a beached whale.

David Foster tried to shake himself to his senses. He realized the smell of diesel fuel and the settling dust was suffocating him. He coughed hard, struggling for breath and choking. He smelled smoke . . . a fire somewhere. What remained of his senses told him he had to get away from the rig before it exploded. He scrambled for his backpack and the Ruger. Where was the Ruger? He couldn't leave it. The smoke was thicker now, more pungent. Foster knew the rig was going to blow. His vision faded in and out, and his senses, his reasoning, came and went quickly. Blow? Not likely. No, not diesel fuel. It would burn, but it wasn't likely to explode or was it the other way around? Did gasoline burn and diesel fuel explode? Foster couldn't think clearly enough to remember. But it really didn't matter because a fire was a fire and gasoline or burning diesel fuel would carry with it a dismal, flaming death.

Foster looked at Glen Hawthorn sprawled haphazardly on the bottom of the rig on what would be the driver's door. On the right side of Hawthorn's face beside his nose, he saw a small hole with blood oozing from it. A hit. The Ruger had done the job well. But then there was more blood from cuts and lacerations across Hawthorn's forehead and cheek. And his left arm was twisted at a distorted angle behind his back. Foster was satisfied the driver was dead. He found his backpack and then the Ruger. David Foster climbed to the top of the rig and, with all his strength, forced the door open. He looked back inside once more at Hawthorn's body. Foster's right hand produced a battered, dried rose from the backpack, and he dropped it onto Hawthorn's mangled body. "Bye, drughead."

In a rush of satisfaction, he felt his senses coming back stronger by the second. He cleared the doorway and climbed onto the side of the cab to make his escape from the scene of his retribution. When the door fell closed, Foster briefly noted the name painted on it: LEECO FREIGHT LINES.

Chapter Seven

Darkness had settled over Dallas when Marc drove the customized overroad war machine through the terminal gate at Leeco Freight Lines. He and Carl expected to have Brittin's report from the FBI laboratory before the night was over. And if that report came back with verification of what the Highway Warriors expected, then a serial killer roamed somewhere in America stalking truckers.

Carl broke the silence. "Looks like Dallas is calm and quiet for once. It's good to see Leeco rebuilt. It looks like a real business again."

Marc came back to the moment as the two Highway Warriors assessed the terminal grounds through the windshield. "I remember once, not too long ago, when the smoke and charred rubble had this place looking like a war zone. I guess, in a way, it *was* a war zone."

Carl stretched his arms. "You know, bro, the entire country is like that. Well, to a lesser extent anyway. It may not always look like a war zone, but under the surface there is a very real enemy."

Marc sat for a long moment, his mind filling with bitter memories. He knew the dark face of the enemy all too well, the face that had taken his mother and uncle and left his father in a coma that seemed to know no end. And it had been those horrid events of what now seemed like a lifetime ago that had caused him and Carl to accept the President's offer to combat the menace on its own ground—using no rules, no restraints. Now the kettle was brewing with the ingredients of still another battle in the war to wipe the scourge from the face of the earth. Yes, Marc Lee knew the enemy all right. And in each battle the faces changed, but the enemy was still the same—the doers of evil destroying lives of innocents. "You're right, the enemy is out there. He's everywhere, in Every City, USA. Sometimes he may only be visible to the trained eye or the victim, but he's definitely out there. While innocent people go on about their daily lives, the scum is plotting, planning, and stalking. Too bad we can only take on one at a time. Too bad there aren't more like you and me. If there was, maybe we could make a difference before it's too late. Before this monster consumes us."

Carl looked at his crime-fighting partner. "Damn, you're talkin' heavy this evening. You okay?"

Marc managed a smile to mask the pain he felt from his own victimization. But he knew that was unnecessary. If there was one person in the world he could talk to with absolute honesty, that person was Carl Browne. "Yeah, I'm okay. Every time I drive back into this lot and see this terminal, I go through it all over again. It's like a living nightmare that doesn't go away. I see my father, Jill, the terminal in flames and shambles . . . it all comes back. Worst part is, I feel every bit of the hurt with a renewed intensity when my mind relives it. You ever go through that when you think about your grandmother?"

Carl returned the smile and looked hard at his closest friend. "Sure. It's normal. Time heals the wound, but the scar tissue never leaves. It means you're human like the rest of us."

"Sometimes that's a hell of a thing to be—human, I mean. Sometimes it hurts mighty bad."

Carl could tell the mental anguish Marc was feeling was just part of the savage brutality of victimization. "I won't tell you any of it will ever go away, but I can tell you it'll hurt a little less with the passing of time. You got to give it time."

Marc made a sweeping glance around the Leeco terminal lot and shrugged his shoulders. "Yeah, you're right. Let's go inside and see if anyone we know is still here. What say?"

"You got it."

The Warriors climbed from the cab of the Leeco rig and went inside the terminal. Winston Andrews, the man sent by the president to operate Leeco until Marcus Lee recovered, was the only person remaining in the office. On the docks it was a different story. The dock foreman and a full crew of at least three dozen dock workers moved freight feverishly from one open trailer to another. Marc smiled at the sight because it reminded him of the Leeco Freight Lines that existed before the beginning of the struggle to smother a raging criminal fire.

Marc looked at the men working and then at Carl. "That's the way I remember Leeco. This is how it was when I sweated on these docks during high school. My father would be proud of the rebirth."

Carl returned the smile. "See, I told you. Now that's the right attitude to have. Think positive."

"Let's go talk to Winston and catch up on the last few days. If it isn't too late when we finish here, I'd like to go see my father before we settle in for the night. It's been a while."

Carl nodded and followed Marc from the dock area to the office. When they got inside the office, Winston Andrews was sitting at a desk talking on the telephone. Both Warriors immediately noticed that Andrews, usually cheery and red-faced, was unusually pale. They stopped and waited for Andrews to complete his call.

Andrews hung up the phone and looked at the Highway Warriors. "Marc, we've lost a driver."

Marc looked hard at Andrews. "What? What do you mean?"

"He's been killed in a traffic accident in Arkansas. That was the state police office from Arkansas. One of our rigs went out of control on U.S. Seventy-one north of Texarkana, left the road, and overturned. The driver was killed. It was Glen Hawthorne."

Marc had immediate flashbacks. Drivers dying. Unexplained accidents. Segalini . . . the mob. "Was there any indication of what happened besides that?"

Andrews took a deep breath. "Yes, I'm afraid so. The state trooper investigating the crash said it appears the driver was shot in the face at close range. When they found his body in the rig, he had a dried rose lying on his chest. What's happening, Marc? What could that mean?"

Marc's face flushed with rage. The veins in his temples swelled. Carl stood beside him and drew a noticably deep breath. Marc looked at Carl. Both Highway Warriors' faces were chisled in stone, hard with no expression.

Marc turned to Winston Andrews. "I'll tell you what it means, Winston. One thing—war!"

———

At first David Foster had been disoriented from the beating he had taken inside the cab and the impact of the crash. But it hadn't taken long for him to regain his senses. He knew despite his temporary trauma, he had to get away from the scene of the crash. He hadn't expected the drug-using driver to be so defensive. None of the others had been. Foster realized his kind of mission entailed certain hazards. He had accepted those hazards in order to fulfill his self-appointed charge. Hawthorn's actions, however, had caught him completely off guard. He mentally critiqued his performance and realized he should have waited for the driver to stop the rig somewhere before he made an attempt to purge him from society.

Apparently the stalled car on the highway had been abandoned. That meant there hadn't been any eyewitnesses to the crash and that was good. At least none Foster had seen. As soon as he had climbed from the rig, he scanned the area around the crash. Smoke rolled from the rig, but he had finally determined it was coming from leaking oil spilling onto the hot engine. There had been no fire and that too was good. It gave him time to get back to the highway before too much attention was called to the wreckage.

Once on the road, David Foster tried to put as much distance as he could between himself and the wreck. He had gotten a half-mile from the crash and hiked his thumb into the air. Even before he heard the sirens coming futilely to the aid of the druggie in the big rig, Foster had gotten another ride.

Reluctantly he had accepted a ride with a southbound driver in a pickup truck. That ride had uneventfully taken him to Texarkana. He had politely thanked the old man who let him off near the edge of the border city. Foster had chosen his departure point with care: there was a truckstop sign within sight. He hadn't wanted the driver to know where he was headed.

He sat there now, sipping coffee and devouring a bacon, lettuce, and tomato sandwich. A Dallas newspaper lay in front of him on the table. Drivers and travelers milled around the truckstop almost lackadaisically. David Foster occasionally looked away from his sandwich and inspected the countless faces roaming around him. It required a vast psychological adjustment to be in the presence of so many people. His self-imposed isolation in the Ozarks had changed his temperament and reduced his tolerance of people. At times he found himself feeling uncomfortable, nervous. He attributed that to the nature of his mission because he knew there were people who would be looking for him soon. He constantly scrutinized his own behavior to ensure that his actions would never call attention to himself. It required a constant mental effort, but thus far he thought he had been successful. He came off as just another hitchhiker seeking a brief sabbatical from the toils of life on the blacktop.

As he assessed the faces of men and women he pinpointed as truck drivers, Foster wondered how many of them were using chemical substances that altered their reflexes and judgment. How many of them were walking time bombs waiting to explode at some inopportune moment and snuff out innocent lives? His only satisfaction was in knowing that now there were fewer threats on the highway. He took solace in his mission. He had vowed that once he eliminated enough truckers to put a dent in the drug users, he would start with drivers of passenger cars. He knew he couldn't get them all, but he would take as many as he could before society overtook him. And he knew eventually they would.

Foster looked back to the newspaper, and an article caught his attention. He read it carefully, then reread it. A new federal law was now in effect, one that required all commercial carriers to hold a valid commercial driver's license. In order to obtain that license, drivers were required to submit to drug and alcohol tests. Opponents were saying it was a violation of their constitutional rights. Foster slammed the paper down and mumbled to himself as he filled with rage. *What about the constitutional rights of my family, huh? What about that?*

He realized he was attracting attention to himself. Foster settled down. Even as he did, he could feel his blood pressure sinking and his heart rate slowing. He picked up his coffee and took a sip. When he set the cup back down he shyly looked around the restaurant to see if anyone was looking at him. They weren't. He breathed another sigh of relief.

Two truck drivers—one tall, lanky, and dark; the other heavier with a modest growth of beard—approached the table directly behind him and sat down. Foster watched the reflection of the men in a nearby window and listened as they talked.

The tall, lanky man spoke. "It's gettin' harder and harder to make a living out on the road these days, Pedal Pusher. The harder I run the more it costs. I drive until

I'm ready to drop and then I have to take those damned old pills to stay awake. I'm startin' to wonder if it's worth it."

The man with the beard hesitated a minute. "I'll tell you what, Bean Pole, it is gettin' tougher. By the way, my name's Larry Cummings. I guess we can drop the CB handles since we're sittin' face to face."

Bean Pole chuckled, then replied, "Billy Edwards. Nice to meet you, Larry. You get out here on the superslab talkin' on the CB and next thing you know you talk like that all the time. Guess sometimes we forget we all have names besides the ones we use on the two-way."

David Foster could see the image of the two men in the window reach over the table and shake hands. But that motion barely registered in his mind. The name . . . Larry Cummings. He knew he had to get a better look at the guy. He also knew there couldn't be too many men named Larry Cummings driving a truck. Foster smiled to himself through his rage. Maybe, just maybe, Lady Luck had tapped his shoulder with her magic wand. He listened.

Cummings looked around the restaurant before he spoke. "If it weren't for pills and truckstop lizards, I wouldn't be worth a shit on the superslab. I stay gone for a month or two at a time. Man's got to have something to keep him awake and some nookie to keep him alive. Lizards ain't the best, but they're better than nothing at all. Whatta you think?"

Edwards chuckled softly. "Not me, man. Truckstop lizards scare the hell outta me. I figure you can get AIDS and a few other diseases that ain't even been discovered yet. I'll get mine where I know it's safe."

Cummings laughed. "Take precautions, man. That's what rubbers are made for. It's like buying pills, you gotta have faith. Way I look at it, everybody's gonna die from something. Either a damned four-wheeler's gonna pull in front of you and stop out on the superslab or you can screw yourself to death. Me, I'll take the last one."

"You're right about that. Damned four-wheelers will get you killed. They got no respect for a big truck."

"Tell me. I smacked one up in Ohio a couple years back. Cost me fifteen months in the big house. Gave me hell when I tried to get my license back. I finally had to get a brand new one out of Idaho. It makes a hell of a mess when a big truck smacks a four-wheeler. It's about like a bulldozer runnin' over a tricycle. Splat!" Cummings laughed.

David Foster fought to contain his rage. He felt his blood pressure skyrocket, and he trembled. He talked to himself silently because he knew he had to take his time. This was neither the time nor the place to requite his agony so he fought his initial urges and kept listening. As he listened he reached into his backpack and removed the tattered newspaper photograph of the man who had slaughtered his wife and children two years before. He looked at it, careful to conceal it from anyone who might be watching him. For several minutes Foster stared at the man's image. It had been burned on his mind, but he didn't want to waste his best treatment on the wrong druggie. Not this time. It had to be right, and now, to confirm it, all he had to do was get a good look at the man sitting back to back with him less than three feet away. And if what the man said was accurate and the face and photograph matched, it was time. But first he had to have an infallible plan.

———

Marc fired instructions at Winston Andrews. "I want everything there is to know in the company files about Glen Hawthorn. I want his driving record, performance evaluations, even his first application for employment. When you have all of that, I want a copy of his complete medical history since he's been with Leeco. I'm especially interested in his company physicals, urine and blood tests, and a complete case history on any and all medical claims that might have been filed through our company's medical insurance program. If there is a prescription record included with the medical insurance program, I want to know every pill that man ever bought through his insurance. Can you have that for me in thirty minutes?"

Winston Andrews felt cool beads of perspiration on his forehead. He hesitated, then digested everything Marc Lee had just said. It was a tall order. He pursed his lips and took a deep breath. "You got it. Remember, I may not know where everything is unless all of the records are in Hawthorn's personnel file or in the computer data base. I'll give it my best shot."

Marc forced a plastic smile. It wasn't Winston's reply that upset him, it was the insurgence of more evil into the Leeco family. "Thanks, Winston."

Andrews hesitated again before he spoke. "Marc, do you suspect Hawthorn was into something he shouldn't have been? I guess what I'm asking is, you suspect he was into drugs? Your requests seem more than just a little slanted toward that."

"I want to be sure there is no mistake and I want to be sure Leeco is clean on this one. I want to eliminate every possibility before we charge off on the wrong foot. Specifically, yes, I am looking for drugs."

Andrews thumbed through some papers on the desk in front of him. "Marc, every driver in this company is subjected to a mandatory drug test at least every three months. Anyone who works here is subject to a spot drug test at any time without notice. I'm not saying someone couldn't have messed up, but Hawthorn was over fifty years old. He isn't your stereotypical drug user. If he was thirty, maybe. I haven't been here long enough to learn all of the employees personally, but I met Hawthorn once and he seemed to me to be a dedicated family man with a level head. I don't see him as a drug user. Of course, that's just my opinion without looking at the history you requested."

Marc shot a glance at Andrews. "I couldn't agree

more with what you just said. If there is an employee in this company with a drug habit, he or she is a master of deception. We're tough on that and I intend to see we stay that way. If it'll make you feel any better, Winston, I'm not trying to prove Glen Hawthorn was using drugs . . . I'm out to prove he wasn't."

Andrews realized he was now very confused. He shook his head and stood from the chair behind the desk. "Okay, Mr. Lee. Whatever you say. It's your company and you have the final word."

Marc's face turned from settling rage to sadness. "It isn't my company, Winston. It still belongs to my father. I'm only the caretaker until he can return." Marc moved toward the door and then turned back toward Andrews. "And he *will* return!"

Andrews nodded in agreement and disappeared down a hallway.

Marc gave Carl a friendly slap on the back. "Let's take a walk to the rig. I want to contact Brittin. He has a few things I could use too."

Carl broke his silence and moved toward the door beside Marc. "He should be calling us in a little while. Should we wait?"

"I don't think we can afford it. He'll have to put on the phony federal smile quickly. There's something we need and he can get it for us. If we linger, it may be too late."

"Like what?"

"Like the results of the autopsy on Hawthorn. I want to know what that man had running through his veins when he died. If he was dirty, that's one thing. If he comes up clean—and I suspect he will—then whoever is responsible for his death is going to suddenly discover the world isn't big enough to hide in. Whatever it takes, I'll find him, and then all hell is gonna break loose."

Chapter Eight

Billy Edwards and Larry Cummings ordered something to eat. David Foster sat only a few feet away, holding onto every word the truckers said. He had run the possible scenario through his mind at least a million times—a face-to-face confrontation with the man who had killed his family. Now that mental picture had become reality, and Foster still couldn't believe it. He looked hard at the tattered newspaper photograph for several minutes, his stare so vengeful that he wouldn't have been surprised if the piece of paper bearing Cummings's image burst into flames from the heated mental intensity.

The plan. Reality dictated that Foster had to deviate from his original course of retribution. The encounter wasn't supposed to be like this. Never, in all the pain-filled, lonely nights high in the Ozarks, did Foster every suspect he would encounter the brutal thief who had stolen his life from him. He had suspected, even planned, that he would have to hunt the swine down like a wounded animal to fulfill his self-appointed mission. The druggies he had terminated until now were just practice, a way to test his skills before he undertook the actual quest. As he sat at the table, his back so near to the man he hunted and hated that he could almost feel the body heat, David Foster realized how unpredictable fate really was. A truckstop restaurant, however, was not the place to take an eye for an eye. No, there were too many witnesses and too much opportunity for interference. Worse yet, someone completely innocent could be injured or even killed. And if that happened, David Foster realized he would be reduced to the same level as the vermin he sought to eradicate, something he wanted to avoid at any cost. He had no argument with anyone other than inconsiderate, irresponsible dopeheads who operated big trucks.

Foster glanced away from the photograph and into the window at the reflection of Cummings and Edwards behind him. Edwards was talking in between slurps of coffee.

"Where are you headed on this run, Larry?"

Cummings answered quickly. "Chicago. I got a load of computer parts for a manufacturer up there. I say parts, well, actually they're metal cases from a vendor in Houston. They've been a good account to keep the eighteen-wheels rollin'. You understand what I'm talkin' about, don't you?"

"I can dig it. When you got to be there?"

"The day after tomorrow. I should be able to make it with time to spare. I'll take a little something to help the miles go by faster, and I could roll into the dock slip by this time tomorrow. Where are you headed?"

"Big, beautiful Baltimore. I must not be holdin' my mouth right or something. I don't know why I took a Baltimore run. I'd rather take a beating than go through Washington, D.C. Hell of it is, there ain't much way to get around it. About the best I can hope for is to time my arrival in the middle of the night when the traffic's less severe. Washington is like New York City; there is no good time to go through there."

Cummings laughed. "Yeah I got me a grip on some of that, I do. I'll take a run West over one on the East Coast any day of the week. I've driven for hours in the West without traffic congestion or Smokies sittin' at every turnoff. I love it out there."

"Me too. Everywhere 'cept California. California Highway Patrol gets a case of the badass every now and then. When they do that, watch out."

Cummings laughed again. "Don't ever get busted with dope in your big rig out there. I knew a guy once that got hisself caught with some uppers. He didn't have but maybe a dozen or two and he ended up servin' four years. Unmerciful bunch of bastards out there."

The waitress returned with their food order. They stopped the conversation and started eating.

The waitress came to David Foster's table. "Can I get something else for you?"

Foster put on his most pleasant smile. "Yes, please. I'd like some more coffee and maybe a slice of pie. What kind of pie do you have?"

The waitress pointed to a glass cooler rack behind the serving counter. "We got peach, lemon meringue, cherry, coconut, and apple."

"What's good?"

"All of it. I like the coconut and apple, though."

"You talked me into it. Let me have apple. Uh, can you heat it?"

"Sure."

"Good. Apple with a big scoop of vanilla ice cream. Can you do that?"

The waitress wrote in her order pad as she spoke. "No problem. Want some whipped cream to top that off?"

"Why not? I'm easy. Add some whipped cream." Foster still projected his best, most friendly, smile.

"Be back in a minute." The waitress turned and disappeared behind the serving counter into the kitchen.

David Foster went back to the newspaper and waited. Although the paper was spread out on the table in front of him, his thoughts were elsewhere. Five or six minutes passed and the waitress returned. When she put his pie on the table, David Foster had his plan.

Behind him, the two truckers finished their meal. Foster ate feverishly but hardly tasted the pie. He glanced frequently into the window to observe the images of the men. When he saw them slip from the table and stand to leave, Foster did the same thing. He slid his chair back hard and grabbed his backpack from the chair next to him. When he turned to leave, he bumped hard into Larry Cummings.

Foster jumped back and spoke apologetically as he analyzed Cumming's face. "Hey, man, I'm sorry. I didn't know you were behind me. I should watch where I'm going."

Cummings was surprisingly pleasant about the whole thing. "That's cool. No problem. You a hiker?"

Foster played shy. "Yeah. I'm headin' up north and thought I'd go outside and try to get a ride before it got too late."

Cummings flipped a toothpick back and forth in his mouth and fumbled with his dinner check. "Where you headed up north?"

"Actually, I'm trying to get to Chicago. Right now, I'd take anything I could find in that direction."

Cummings smiled. "Well hell's bells, boy, I'm headed for Chicago myself. If you don't fart more than I do or snore louder than I do, I'd welcome your company. Name's Larry Cummings."

Foster tried to appear grateful. He smiled and extended his right hand. "Puckett. Donald Puckett. Most everybody calls me Don. I sure would welcome the ride. You sure it won't put you out?"

"Hell, no. If I got somebody to talk to besides the drivers on the CB, we might make it to Chicago by noon tomorrow. We can get down and do some serious trucking."

"Wow, that would be great. Is it okay if I call you Larry?"

"Sure. Call me Larry or Pedal Pusher. That's my CB handle. I'll answer to either one of 'em. Sometimes I even answer to 'hey you' or 'asshole.' If I don't like who's sayin' it, I just whip their ass." Cummings chuckled and moved away from the table. "Let's pay these checks and do some truckin'. By the way, this here is Billy Edwards."

Foster acknowledged Edwards with a nod of his head and shuffled the backpack onto his shoulder. "Boy, what a stroke of luck. I can't believe you're headed to the same place I am. I must be livin' right or something."

Cummings smiled again. "Well, if you ain't, you will be by the time me and you get to Chicago." His voice dropped to a whisper. "You got any smoke in that pack of yours?"

Foster was caught off guard. "You a narc or what?"

"Shit. Me? I'm a lot of things, but a narc ain't one of 'em."

Foster smiled, a wave of intense pleasure flowing through him. "In that case, I got something better than any smoke. You give me a ride and I'll give you a trip unlike anything you've ever had. I guarantee it."

———

Brittin Crain knew the markings of a serial killer when he saw them. With more than ten years of law enforcement and criminal investigations under his belt, Crain had developed the knack of spotting both the obvious and the latent leads that developed from thorough investigations. His position at the Department of Justice gave him great leverage in utilizing the massive investigative machinery at his disposal. Not one prone to shyness, Crain seldom hesitated to activate the weapons available to him. But it was that knack, that street-honed sixth sense, that made his contribution to the president's secret war such a tremendous one.

Marc Lee and Carl Browne had a knowledge of war, terrorists, search and destroy, communications, hostage rescue, and the application of force to achieve a designated end; Brittin knew how to manage a criminal investigation. He also knew how to detect the seemingly insignificant things that were oftentimes overlooked by the average guy behind a badge. Together, the Highway

Warriors and the FBI liaison made a tough team for criminals to deal with.

The sixth sense was working overtime now. With the FBI laboratory running every conceivable test on the evidence collected at three murder scenes, Brittin made it his business to gather whatever initial information he could. This case had taken on a new meaning to him. If truckers were the target, then something had to be done and done quickly. Truckers were closer to Brittin Crain than almost any other professionals, except maybe cops. He had practically grown up in the Lee family household. Trucking was their business and their livelihood. Brittin knew if he hadn't decided to become a cop, he would probably have been a truck driver.

The spinning sixth sense and the desire to get a handle on the case caused him to fumble impatiently with a pencil while he waited for the forensic technician at the FBI laboratory to return to the telephone. The lab had initiated its first battery of tests on the dried roses found in two different states at three separate murder scenes. Crain's gut told him there would be a common link, and hopefully the lab analysis would confirm that. Crain was becoming quite antsy, and he mumbled to himself as he cradled the telephone receiver. *Come on, fellow. What's takin' you so long?*

The words had hardly cleared his mouth when he heard the guy pick the phone back up. "Okay, Mr. Crain. I've got the results of the preliminaries. You realize, of course, these are simply our initial test results. We've only had these samples for a few hours. We need more time to positively confirm and reconfirm our test results."

Crain's voice was sharp. "Yes, I understand. Just give me what you have and call me later with the finals."

"All right. The specimens, and we're speaking of the dried flower material when I say specimens, were apparently roses. We cannot estimate the age of the plant substance without further evaluation. My initial hunch is more than one year. Unofficially, of course. They were red roses, species unknown at this stage. Each flower was attached to a slender green wooden rod seven-and-one-half centimeters in length. Wood appears to be balsa or something similar. The stem of the flower was attached to the wooden rod by a section of green wire. These are both materials commonly in use by virtually any and every florist in the country, so that in itself tells us nothing important. What *is* important is that each of the wire sections match in dimension and outward texture as do the wooden rods. That tells us they most likely came from the same florist. When I get a little further into it, I can tell you positively. As it stands, I'm just ninety-nine percent sure. Also, there are sections of latent—"

Crain interrupted. "Hold on a minute. You're telling me these flowers probably came from the same place? Are you also telling me there isn't any way to point them toward one florist or even one specific area of the country?"

The technician, his voice slow, methodical, and nonchalant, answered quickly. "Precisely. If you'll bear with me a moment, I have some other information you may find of interest, because we did. We isolated a residual foreign substance common to each dried flower. That's a polite way of saying dirt. Fine granular particles of dirt were embedded in each specimen. I would call this, for simplicity, aftermarket dirt. By that I mean particles that were caused to adhere to the flowers after they left the florist. In addition to that, we have found small sections of latent fingerprints on the wooden rods, the stems, if you will. I anticipate a saline print recovery analysis as soon as we have finished most of the other tests. Don't bank on finding much from that, though. The small dimensions of the stems will, at best, yield only partial segments of print lines. I wouldn't count on getting much there. Best case, they could be used in a prosecution to confirm the presence of one suspect with possession of the flower. It would be marginal, but better than nothing. The possibility exists that the specimens were handled by people with, shall we say, less than adequate competence prior to our receiving them."

Crain felt juices in his stomach that caused him to feel almost nauseated. "So you're telling me that even if there are recovered print sections, they may be of little value to us because some asshole didn't know what he was doing when they were recovered?"

The technician chuckled. "That about sums it up. But sit tight. I don't think the prints are our most important linkage. There is something else. I should say, a couple of things. Listen to this: Each stem, that is, the wooden rod, bore trace elements of both polycarbonate substances and polystyrene residue. That tells me these stems had been inserted into a Styrofoam or extruded foam holder of some sort. Essentially, these flowers probably came from a wreath of some type or at least a vase with a hard foam insert. From the content and texture of each trace element, analysis reveals they were most likely embedded in the same holder at one time or another. Are you with me on that much?"

Crain took a breath and checked the tape in his cassette recorder beside the telephone to be sure he didn't miss any of the information. "You're saying these roses, were probably in the same vase or a wreath of some kind. What I've got to figure out is when and why. There is a symbolic message here somewhere and I've got to put that link together. What else do you have?"

"Two things that stand out initially. First, I have trace elements of a nylon fabric on two of the specimens. Red, from what I can tell by the dye. It's dirty and difficult to say with certainty. Nylon is a polychromatophilic material, so it will take extensive analysis to ascertain the dye content. What I can tell you now is that the nylon likely came from the same fabric section. That is to say, the same nylon object. What we're speaking of here is something like a travel bag, a tote bag, assault rifle case, or a backpack. Something like that. Everybody and his dog makes them for the open market. You find the bag and I'll verify the flowers were in it, but other than that, I can't point you in any given direction."

Crain was trying to analyze everything the technician said. "You weave an interesting web. You said there was one more thing. Let me have it."

The technician continued in his dry, technical voice. "This one puzzles me. We have isolated microscopic particles on the petals of all three roses. Spores, the best I can tell. My reference materials point to something, but I want to verify it with solid chemical analysis first."

Crain was puzzled. "Spores. Like yeast or something? What kind of spores?"

"You're on the right track. To me, they look like spores from mushrooms. Specifically, I'm guessing Fly Amanita."

Crain almost bit his tongue. "Say that in English so a country boy from Dallas can understand it. What the hell is Fly Amanita?"

The technician chuckled. "Sorry. Fly Amanita is one of the most potent and deadly wild mushrooms known to exist. There is no known antidote for ingestion of its toxins, and it's very fast-acting. That's a nice way of saying that if you get a decent dose of that stuff, your ass is dead."

Crain digested it all. "Where is that mushroom found?"

"All over the country really. Most likely in mountainous regions with heavy forests and a good deal of moisture. Villainous little beast, too. More than one unsuspecting amateur mushroom harvester has met his demise from erroneous identification of the little jewel. By the way, I'll have the identification confirmed by morning, if not before then."

Crain hesitated. "Great. What's your gut feeling on all this?"

"My gut feeling? Well, let's see. I'd say we're dealing with a psychotic serial killer, an outdoorsman who knows his shit. An analysis of the autopsy reports on the three victims will tell me a great deal. I'd also say he's got a hard-on for truckers. I can't exactly decipher the significance of the rose unless it's just his or her trademark. These psycho types do that kind of thing. I would, however, go further and say if he's handling highly toxic mushrooms and he's still alive, this character is very, very dangerous."

———

"Pathfinder to Barnburner, do you copy?" Marc let the Icom microphone drop into his lap after the second call. He looked at Carl, who sat beside him at the console of the Leeco rig's command center in the high-tech trailer. "Wonder where he went?"

Carl grinned. "You know Brittin, he's chasin' something. Give him a minute; he'll answer."

Marc fondled the microphone. "I'll give him one more try, then I'll change frequencies and go into Delta Force Command."

The Icom speaker crackled with a Texas drawl. "Pathfinder, this is Barnburner. Stand by just a minute, ol' buddy. I've got something for you but I need a minute to get my act together."

Marc keyed the microphone. "Roger. Pathfinder standing by on ConSat-D Echo one."

Carl laughed. "See, I told you. He's onto something."

Marc wasn't amused. "Yeah, but what? Is it business or a skirt?"

"Well, Colonel, boys will be boys."

Brittin Crain's voice blared from the speaker. "Pathfinder, this is Barnburner. Are you there?"

Marc pressed the push-to-talk switch and answered, "Waitin' ol' buddy. Go ahead with your traffic."

"I've got some goodies for you. Are you ready to copy?"

"Let me give you something first. We may be onto another one. This one is too close to home. A Leeco driver was found in a traffic accident north of Texarkana a few hours ago. His rig crashed and he was dead. One problem, though. He'd been shot in the face." Marc released the transmit switch and gave Crain a chance to fully comprehend his information.

Brittin replied instantly. "What's the link or is there one?"

"Our flower child may be at it again. They found a dried rose on his body."

Disgust was obvious in Crain's voice when he replied via the ComSat-D satellite link. "Wonderful. Just wonderful."

Marc was anxious to get his request out and to get the wheels of the FBI turning in search of some solid answers. "I've got a chore for you. I want a complete and unabridged copy of the autopsy report just as soon as it's completed. You or your people can get that a lot faster than I can. I want you to intervene with your federal nobility and be sure extensive drug tests are run on the body. I need to know if the driver—his name is Glen Hawthorn—was using anything or if any trace elements of any kind of drug whatsoever show up in the postmortem blood analysis. Can you do that?"

Crain hesitated a few seconds before his voice came from the speaker. "Sure, no sweat. You think the driver was on drugs? Over."

"No, I think if drugs are a link and they're what our killer is seeking, then I think he's screwed up. You know as well as I do that Leeco has an industry-leading drug-testing program. A driver for Leeco would have to have a substitute take his tests before he could get away with taking drugs and still work for the company. My gut tells me the man died clean. Over."

Crain replied immediately. "Consider it done. I'll have everything there is to know as soon as it's available. Now it's my turn. I firmly believe I've got our link. I think our killer is someone who has been greatly harmed by a trucker in the past few years. I'll give you a complete rundown of the data and the test results in just a minute so you can see why I've drawn this conclusion. Off the top of my head I'd say we're after a hitchhiker."

Chapter Nine

Almost three hours had passed since David Foster climbed into the cab of the big eighteen-wheeler with Larry Cummings. They had left the truckstop in Texarkana and were headed east on I-30. Foster felt comfortable with his alias of Don Puckett since he had put a substantial amount of time in researching the name and history of the real Donald Puckett.

Larry Cummings had lived up to his CB handle of Pedal Pusher because he kept the pedal to the metal. The big rig had roared through the night, oblivious to speed limits and the risk of Smoky with radar. High above the instrument console inside the cab sat an Escort radar detector. When the light flashed on and the detector sounded its alarm, Cummings would let off the accelerator and drop below the speed limit until he spotted and passed the source of the alarm. When he had done that, his heavy foot slammed to the floor again.

Conversation had been light, with Cummings talking mostly about how unfairly the police treated truckers. Then, rather than talk to Foster, Cummings had chosen to chit-chat on the CB since the moment he drove the big rig from the truckstop parking lot.

David Foster didn't really care if Cummings didn't talk to him because it gave him an opportunity to review his plan. Thinking of what he had in store for Larry Cummings pleased Foster. He felt no remorse for what was about to happen; instead, he felt a twinge of guilt that the company expecting a load of computer parts was going to be out of luck. Larry Cummings and those parts wouldn't arrive on time and probably never would arrive at all.

Cummings broke the silence between the two men inside the cab. "We'll be in Little Rock soon. You want a bite to eat and a pee break?"

"Sure, why not?"

"Good, there's a truckstop just outside Little Rock. We can coast in there and fill the fuel tanks, the old belly, and drain our bladders. I'm gettin' tired. I could become real interested in that good stuff you said you had if it'll help keep me awake. Will it?"

Foster's beard moved to expose a broad smile. "Like I said, man, it'll give you a feeling you've never had before."

Cummings was excited. "All right! Tell you what, after we break at the truckstop, I'll take a little sample of that stuff if you don't mind."

"Great. You'll find I'm not a greedy man. I'll gladly share my stash with anyone who deserves it. And I think you deserve it."

"Puckett, you're okay, man. I like you. Me and you, well, we're just gonna hammer down and float on in to the Windy City."

Foster decided to try some conversation. "You got it, dude. Say, man, how long you been drivin'?"

"Eight years, give or take a few months. I had a little break for about fifteen months."

"You get pissed and quit or what?"

"A judge up in Ohio sent me on vacation because of a wreck. I'd been snortin' some coke the night before and tappin' a truckstop lizard, and then I took some uppers to keep me flyin'. Flew a little too low and cracked up."

"Wow! Did you get hurt or anything?"

Cummings didn't hesitate to respond. He gripped the steering wheel tightly and kept the rig rolling at over seventy miles per hour. "Naw. I trashed the rig and part of it burned."

Foster controlled himself and pushed further. "Gee, what happened?"

Cummings spoke without remorse. The tone of his voice and the inflections he used made it sound as if he was almost proud of his crash. "Some broad in a van stopped too fast in a construction zone and I creamed her. Judge gave me some time, but I got out in fifteen months cause I'm such a nice guy. Damned four-wheelers just got no respect for a big truck. Hell, man, they gotta learn that we rule the road. We're bigger and heavier than they are. We pay a hell of a lot more highway taxes than they do. We're out here on the highway to make a living, not to toot around on a friggin' vacation or something. Those four-wheelers piss me off, I'll tell you. It's a damned shame we don't have roads just for big trucks."

Foster struggled with his emotions to keep from killing the dopehead instantly. His better judgment told him no and he listened to it. All things in good time, he thought to himself. "Sounds like you really don't like people unless they're in an eighteen-wheeler. What do you drive when you're not working on the road? Don't you drive a four-wheeler?"

"Hell, Puckett. I'm always working on the road. I got me a pick'em-up truck that I drive sometimes. But I guarantee you one damned thing, I don't drive on the road like some of those crazy people in four-wheelers. No way. I'm a professional."

Foster smiled a forced, plastic smile. "I can see that by the way you handle this truck. You've probably put some hard miles behind you, haven't you?"

Cummings laughed. "You got a good attitude, Puckett. You're damned straight. I've put some hard and heavy miles behind me. I'm a damned good driver. I drive hard, work hard, and get the loads there on time. In the process, I make me an almost decent living. Ain't that what it's all about?"

"I wouldn't know for sure. I've met a good many

drivers out here on the open highway. Some of them think like you do and some have other opinions. I guess it's all in how you envision the question."

Cummings's voice grew angry. "I ain't real sure what you just said. You sayin' I'm wrong about the way I think?"

Foster thought fast and shot back. "Oh, no. I'm not saying that at all. That's not what I meant. I know you're out here to make a living and get the loads there on time. I suppose if I had to contend with some of the things you guys do out here, I wouldn't last too long. You got the police layin' for you and cars to deal with. Wow. I don't know how you do it. I admire truckers." Foster hoped that settled his error. He realized he had almost blown it, so he decided to choose his words more carefully before he got the druggie pissed enough to throw him out of the cab. He was much too far now to allow this opportunity to slip through his fingers.

Cummings settled and his voice returned to normal. "Good, I thought you was too nice a guy to see things the wrong way. People just don't understand us truckers, that's all. We're underpaid and overworked and we got nobody to speak for us. It's tough on us most times. Hell, boy, truckin's my livin'. If I don't haul freight, I don't eat. I kinda gotten myself partial to eatin'. You know what I mean?"

Foster played into the man's hands. "Damn straight. I understand. I hope you didn't take me too wrong. I didn't mean anything by what I said. I really do realize it's tough on you guys. Tell you what, just to show my good faith, I'll buy the next hot meal. What say?"

Cummings mellowed quickly now. "That's damned decent of you. Hell, I'll just take you up on it. After we eat a bite, I still want to try some of your good stuff. Deal?"

Foster smiled when he realized he had conquered his prey. "You got yourself a deal, Pedal Pusher. Like I said, it's top of the line and superfine."

Cummings slapped the steering wheel. "Yeah! I got me a grip on some of that, I do. Truckstop is just ahead. We ought to be there in a few minutes cause I'm hammer down."

Foster grinned again. "Right on, good buddy!"

Cummings shot back, "Hey, watch that good-buddy shit. You know what a good buddy really is, don't you?" He laughed.

"Well, maybe I don't. What is it?"

Cummings was laughing hysterically now. "Well, I'll tell you. A good buddy, he be a guy that goes into town and gets himself two blow-jobs, and then he comes back and gives you one."

Foster forced a laugh. "Maybe I'd better can the good-buddy crap. I guess I never had much of an opportunity to catch on to all that radio talk."

Cummings was still laughing. "Yeah, when you're talkin' trash it pays to know what you're talkin' about. You can always tell when the driver of a four-wheeler is playin' with his radio. Assholes don't usually know what they're sayin'. It gets funny sometimes."

Foster let the laugh drop. "I can see that it would. How much farther to the truckstop?"

Cummings pointed out the windshield. "There's the exit right in front of us. Two minutes until we shut her down and grab some grub."

David Foster stared out the windshield and saw the truckstop sign towering above the highway. "Good deal. I'm ready for some chow."

Cummings shifted lanes and slowed the rig to exit when the sign came into full view. They rolled to a stop at the end of the exit ramp as Cummings worked the clutch, shifted gears, and pressed on the brake. When Cummings accelerated and moved onto the access high-way toward the truckstop, David Foster moved his hand into the side pocket of his backpack and wrapped his fingers around the grip of the Ruger automatic. The feel of the weapon gave him renewed courage. He knew it was almost time.

———

Marc and Carl had decided the solution to Hawthorn's death didn't lie in Dallas. The most logical place to initiate a search for the man's killer was from a point near the scene of the crime. Being professionals, Marc and Carl both realized logic seldom governed the criminal mind, and that made tracking a random killer even more difficult. Right now the path to the killer was as broad as it was long, and the possibility of more than one killer couldn't be ruled out. With the increasing menace of cults, street gangs, and drug cartels loose on American soil, the realm of possibilities was endless. But somewhere a sick mind or sick minds wandered freely and that had to stop. Permanently.

In Washington, the silent sleuth, liaison, and friend, Brittin Crain, sought answers that would link together the pieces of an increasingly mysterious puzzle, one that only hours before had been little more than a news clip in a trucking magazine. But now the harvest of the grim reaper's scythe had fallen too close to home. Leeco and everyone who worked there was family; if the dismal harvester had snatched away an innocent life then the perpetrator had to be brought to justice. Soon, perhaps the results of an autopsy on Glen Hawthorn's body would reveal the specifics of his death and the secrets of his life. If there were any. Until then, or until some shred of evidence pointed him in the proper direction, searching for the random killer was equivalent to searching for a specific grain of sand in the ocean surf. And the likelihood of a successful solution diminished with each moment the killer had to distance himself from the scene of his evil deed.

The Highway Warriors had been on the road for over an hour since their conversation with Crain. They drove north toward southern Arkansas, headed for the last known position of the killer. And although the tracks would have surely cooled, it was a starting place.

The cab of the Leeco rig had been silent since Marc drove from the terminal lot at Leeco Freight Lines in Dallas. Both men went over the known facts, skimpy as they were, again and again in their minds, searching for a thread that would lead them through the tangled web. The Delta Force warriors turned Highway Warriors had served through enough hells together to understand that verbal communication wasn't always a necessity. Sometimes silence served as the best communicator, and time spent in silent mental analysis yielded the most productive end results.

Finally Carl spoke. "Something I can't seem to piece together, bro. If the killer or killers is leaving his trademark and that trademark is a dead, dried rose, what's he tellin' us?"

Marc didn't answer for a moment. "Bottom line is, best I can determine, the character wants to get caught, and he wants to be damned sure he gets credit for his work."

Carl rubbed his chin and spoke slowly. "Yeah, I understand that. But what is he *tellin'* us? Why a dead, dried rose? Why not a fresh one? There's got to be something symbolic about it somewhere and we're missin' it. I think it's more than a trademark."

Marc hesitated. "You're right, no doubt about it. Maybe the tests Brittin and the federal boys are running at the lab will tell us something. There's a message there, concealed in the dried petals of those flowers, if only we could figure it out. Maybe the killer is a florist or a mortician or maybe just some psycho with a flower fetish. Question is, why truckers? Why so long between these deaths? Didn't the article say it had been a three-month period?"

Carl grew cold-faced. "You may take this as funny, but it's not intended that way. Could it be we're on to a woman killer with real bad PMS, and she only kills once a month?"

Marc didn't laugh. "Stranger things have happened. I read a report the other day that said violent crime was up five and a half percent over last year. With the criminal beast devouring this country, anything could happen. Sad part is, almost every time it happens another innocent life is lost. It's a shame the dirtbags couldn't start doing like the gangsters of the Roaring Twenties did and just kill each other."

Carl snapped back. "Wait a minute . . . something just clicked."

"What?"

"What you just said about killing each other. Didn't the report say all of the truckers showed a sign of drugs in their systems?"

"Yeah."

Carl grinned. "Play this scenario. We got a killer who has a big hard-on for druggies . . . truckers who take drugs. And this killer is playin' a game, maybe a hitchhiker, maybe not. He goes after the trucker druggies—and he's cleaning up the industry, one body at a time. Does it wash?"

Marc contemplated the idea for a moment. "Some of it does. It leaves another barrage of questions, though. Why truckers and not just the dealers on the street corner? Were all of the victims on the stuff? Was Glen Hawthorn smart enough and desperate enough to evade Leeco's stringent drug-testing program? And if that's the case, how does this killer or killers select the next victim?"

Carl sat silent for a moment. "Could it be that this killer is taking out people other than truckers and nobody has made the connection yet?"

Marc nodded his head as he steered the Leeco rig over the highway. "Could be. Like I said before, right now anything is possible. We can sit here and speculate all day, but until we have something solid to move on, we're running blind."

Brittin Crain's voice across the Icom speaker brought the conversation to a halt. "Pathfinder, this is Barnburner on F-four. You out there, boys?"

Carl reached for the microphone. "Go ahead, Brittin."

The speaker crackled again. "Ah, such a changing world we live in. Got your request in to the proper people in Arkansas. We should have something by morning from the postmortem exam. At the Bureau's request, a team of evidence technicians are gonna do their number on the cab of the truck. Hopefully, everybody and his cow hasn't been fumbling around inside the wreckage. What's new on your end?"

Carl pressed the push-to-talk switch. "Dark skys and white lines. We're rolling toward Arkansas as we speak. We'd like to take a look for ourselves. Discreetly, of course."

"Affirmative. Since you're sitting down, I'll give you the latest scoop from the bowels of the federal system. We got us another body."

Marc looked at Carl and both men stared at each other for several seconds. "Where?"

"Outside of Fort Smith. Trademark's the same. One dead truck driver and one dead rose. Arkansas state police are on the scene now. Found the poor bastard twisted into a knot from seizures. No initial marks or injuries, but just as dead. The rig was sitting in a rest area with the driver in the front of the cab. I've requested the full inside line on this one also."

Marc held out his hand and Carl handed the Icom microphone to him. Marc pressed the switch and spoke. "How long ago?"

Crain's voice projected clearly from the satellite-linked radio speaker. "Got the word when I called the powers that be in Arkansas. They found the stiff about an hour ago. Those Arkansas people are starting to get real nervous. Trooper on the scene remembers checking a hitchhiker a few hours before the body turned up. May not be anything to it, but I got all the info from the folks out there. Lucky for us, the dispatcher logged the Social Security number the officer gave him. I'm running all of that through the big beast computer to see what she regurgitates. Guy's name was Donald Puckett."

———

David Foster had grown very irritated with Larry Cummings during their meal. Foster wasn't really hungry, but the stop presented an opportunity he couldn't pass up. Foster was ready to shut the loud-mouthed truck driver up once and for all. Once they returned to the rig outside the truckstop restaurant, Cummings climbed into the lair like a moth drawn to a flickering candle.

Cummings was overly eager. "All right, my man. Thanks for the chow. I'm ready to dip into your stash and try some of that good shit you been tellin' me about. Are we on?"

Foster smiled. "You got it, dude. The primo product is on the way." Foster removed a foil package slightly larger than a book of matches from his backpack. He methodically unwrapped the little package. Then he took a caplet from it and held it between his fingers.

Cummings eyed the caplet. "That's mighty good shit, huh?"

"It'll give you a feeling like nothing you ever had. Best part is, it comes with a money-back guarantee."

Cummings wasn't sure what to say. "I thought you said this one was payment for the ride—a freebie?"

"It is. That's why it comes with a money-back guarantee." Foster laughed, and from the corner of his eye he saw Cummings do the same thing.

Cummings held up a partially empty coffee cup. "Put it on me. I got just enough coffee left to sink the beauty down the hatch."

Foster smiled and passed the red caplet to Cummings. The driver looked at it briefly and plopped it into his mouth. He followed it with a big gulp of coffee, and the pill slipped down his throat.

Foster kept smiling. "Easy, huh?"

Cummings wiped his mouth and grinned also. "What did you say that stuff is called?"

"Red Rocket, 'cause it fires you off and sends you out of this world."

Cummings laughed. "I like it. Red Rocket, huh? That's cool."

David Foster had already initiated his mental timing. He knew the effects of the drug would soon become apparent, and he wanted to see the look on Cummings's face when they did. More satisfying than the hunt was the look of the prey when it was finally conquered into involuntary submission. Foster treasured that last instant when the druggie knew he'd been had.

It came.

Cummings was unsteady in his seat now, nodding sideways and then toward the steering wheel. He was trembling. His words were slurred. "Wh-attt's in this st-uff? Wow! Weird, man."

Foster smiled and watched the show.

"Ah, pain. Oh!" Cummings grabbed at his chest. His breathing became labored. "What have you . . . done . . . to . . . me?" Cummings's eyes opened wide in horror. His mouth hung open involuntarily, gasping for breath. His hands beat frantically at his chest and then fell limp at his side.

Foster grinned, the Ruger automatic in his right hand now. "I gave you what you wanted, asshole. A trip. You're blasting off on a one-way trip and the ride has only started."

Chapter Ten

David Foster savored the appearance of terror on Larry Cummings's face. The shock, the horror, gave him a rush of satisfaction. At last, he felt a sense of relief. For now, Foster knew, justice would settle in on the man responsible for the death of his family more than two years ago. Now the man who took drugs, drove a speeding overroad rig, and crashed into an innocent family snuffing out their lives would get a dose of retribution. And from the repayment of that lethal debt, there just might come a flag of caution to all like him who jeopardized innocent lives daily by virtue of their unconscionable, selfish actions.

When Cummings's eyes finally closed and his entire body fell limp, as his arms had seconds earlier, Foster made his move. He lowered the Ruger .22 auto and put it away inside his backpack. Then he climbed over the area separating the seats in the cab and grabbed Cummings's arms, tugging until the sleeping trucker's body moved. Once he had Cummings in the passenger's seat, he strapped him in with the seat belt and climbed back to the driver's seat.

Foster fired the rig and worked the clutch. The big overroad rig moved forward, sluggishly at first but then smoothly. Foster gained speed and left the truckstop parking lot. After a few minutes on the road, he found himself handling the rig like a real professional. He had already plotted his course in his mind while he ate with Cummings at the truckstop. Now all that stood between him and the final completion of his mission was white lines on Interstate 40.

Mile markers clicked by with clockwork precision as Foster moved the rig toward Russellville. He drove just under or at the speed limit. There were two reasons for that. First, it wouldn't attract attention to him or the rig. Second, he felt it wasn't safe for either himself or the motoring public to run the rig like a hell-bound cowboy.

Cummings slept peacefully in the passenger's seat. Foster expected the druggie trucker to continue a peaceful, tranquil sleep for the next eighteen to twenty-four hours. The drug mixture he had given Cummings had been a near overdose of diazepam and vitamin C with red food coloring. He had concocted the mixture from left over tranquilizers given to him by his doctor immediately after the death of his family. He had chosen not to use them, so he had tucked them away for a later day. The mountains had given him many hours to scheme and dream for his final retribution. The original tablets from the doctor's prescription had been dissolved, dried, and reinserted into the vitamin C caplet. As a final touch to give the preparation a homemade appearance, he had covered it with drops of water-soluble red food coloring. Larry Cummings's sleeping body was living proof of the effectiveness of the compound.

White lines continued to drift by, and David Foster felt more exhuberation from the sweet taste of victory. The taste grew even sweeter because he knew the very best was yet to come. Death would come for the druggie responsible for his family's annihilation, yes, but it would come slowly and deliberately. And he knew he would soon be the master of the man who had not only taken the life of his wife, his son, and his daughter, but his life, too. The result of his loss would be the termination of Larry Cummings. An eye for an eye. Once he had satisfied his palate for revenge, Larry Cummings would receive what he and every druggie like him deserved.

Foster knew that once he reached the Blazer and made it to the mountains, there was nothing on earth to stop his insatiable desire for sweet revenge.

The miles from Little Rock to Russellville had gone by quickly. Foster slowed the rig slightly when he passed the exit warning sign a mile from the Russellville exit. When he reached the exit, he rolled off of Interstate 40, made the turn, and headed for the small strip shopping center where he had left the Chevrolet Blazer.

There was almost no traffic in the middle of the night in Russellville. Foster drove unobstructed to the shopping center and stopped the overroad rig beside the Blazer.

His senses were keyed up now, his brain on full alert. First, he looked around the center to be sure there were no other people there. He saw no one and that was good. Even the all-night restaurant appeared empty. Next, he scanned the Blazer to be sure it hadn't been tampered with or vandalized. It, too, looked clean. He reached in his backpack and removed the little Ruger .22 auto. It was standard operating procedure to have a round in the chamber, so Foster didn't bother to check it. He tucked the weapon inside his faded jeans at the waistband and tugged his shirttail out until it covered the gun.

One more look at Larry Cummings to be sure the murderous truck driver was still out cold and Foster climbed from the cab of the eighteen-wheeler. He made a quick walk-around inspection of the area. Like before, it was clear and calm. Next, he moved to the Blazer. He pulled the keys from his pocket and unlocked the door. Inside, a blue tarp lay folded behind the rear seat. He took it out and laid it on the floor in front of the back seat.

Foster went back to the overroad rig. He climbed the step and opened the passenger's door. A quick nudge into Cummings's side indicated the man was still sleeping like a passed-out drunk. He leaned across Cummings and grabbed his backpack. David Foster realized the only viable enemy he had now was time, so he moved quickly. He opened the backpack and removed two small timer-activated incendiary devices made from homemade chemical compounds. He took one in each hand and went to the fuel tanks on each side of the rig. Next, he enclosed each timer in a zip-top plastic bag and unscrewed the filler cap from the fuel tank. Setting the timers through the plastic bag didn't prove to be a problem, and in seconds both ignition devices were armed and counting. Foster slid one device into each fuel tank, saving the driver's side for last, and replaced the filler cap. No need to worry about fingerprints because the fire would surely take care of that, so he walked swiftly back to the passenger's door.

As he lifted the backpack and moved toward the Blazer, Foster caught a glimpse of headlights turning into the shopping center. His heart raced and his first thought was, *A cop.*

It wasn't.

A small pickup truck approached the front of the shopping center and drifted along in front of the shops throwing something out at each one.

A newspaper delivery boy.

Foster breathed a sigh of relief and went on about his business, when suddenly the headlights glared down on him. He looked toward them and then away to save anything that might be left of his vision. The driver of the little pickup moved toward him. When he got in front of the Blazer, the guy stopped and David Foster fought off the panic.

The man yelled from the pickup. "Want a paper?"

Foster hesitated, trying to catch his breath. He glanced toward Larry Cummings sleeping in the passenger's seat in plain view of the delivery boy. "Uh, sure. How much?"

"On the house. I got plenty."

Foster moved toward the little truck and reached

out to accept the offering. "Thanks. I need to catch up on what's happening in the world."

The driver, a young man in his late teens, laughed. "I don't know if it'll take too much catchin' up. It's the same. shit, just a different day."

Foster glanced at the front page and nodded in agreement. "Yeah, I suppose it is."

The delivery boy pointed at Cummings. "What's the matter with him? He sleeping?"

"Yeah. Son of a bitch sleeps like a rock. He'll be pissed when I wake him in a few minutes."

"Looks more like he's dead."

Foster was caught very much off guard, but he hid it well. "No such luck. I'll have to put up with him another day. When he wakes up and realizes I drove all the way here, he'll wish he was dead. Hard to get good help these days."

The delivery boy stretched his arms and yawned. "Yeah. I gotta go. Enjoy the paper."

Foster felt another burst of relief. "Sure, thanks."

The driver waved, dropped the little truck into reverse, and moved away.

David Foster watched carefully until the driver disappeared at the end of the building. He quickly grabbed the backpack and tossed it into the front of the Blazer. He climbed back into the cab and loosened Cummings's seatbelt, then he let the sleeping trucker fall over his shoulders. When he stepped from the cab, he realized that Cummings weighed more than he had first guessed. He wasn't quite six feet tall, but he probably weighed almost a hundred and seventy pounds.

Moving from the cab to the open door of the Blazer was a chore, but finally Foster made it. He dumped Larry Cummings into the backseat and quickly covered him with the blue tarp. That done, he ran back to the rig, removed the keys, and closed the doors. In seconds, he was in the Blazer. He hit the ignition key and the starter groaned. The engine didn't catch, but it turned over. Foster let off the key and his heart raced. He hit it again and this time, the engine fired.

Foster tapped the accelerator to get the fuel pumping and to permit the engine to warm slightly. When he glanced at his watch he realized all hell was going to erupt in less than three minutes. He shifted into gear and drove away from the doomed overroad rig and all of the physical evidence that could possible link him to Larry Cummings.

It took less than five seconds to get on the road headed north and away from Russellville. Foster felt confident he had made it. Then suddenly he saw blue lights flashing behind him, and the night filled with the sound of a siren.

———

Marc Lee was sure of one thing: when he got to the crash scene of Glen Hawthorn's rig, he would have to be cool and cautious. If the wreckage remained there, and he suspected it would, he would have to tread lightly in making his own investigation to avoid arousing suspicion that he had any interest beyond that of a trucking company representative. Hopefully the evidence technicians requested by Brittin Crain at the Justice Department would do a thorough job of gathering all the evidence linking Hawthorn's tragedy to the suspected crazed killer that had unleashed his vengeance on truckers. But like most situations that required reliance upon the performance of other people, investigations didn't always go the way they should. Marc had learned long ago that it usually paid to ease into the arena personally and leave with his own evaluation. And that was exactly what he and Carl were doing—easing toward the lethal arena.

According to the information furnished by the authorities in Arkansas and the input received from Brittin Crain, the crash site should be very near. Marc expected to see the fringes of a traffic tie-up at any second, but as yet, it hadn't appeared.

Carl was restless. His mind raced with possibilities in the face of another bloody battle to rid the United States of criminal scum. But now, nothing seemed to fit. "I can't get it to jell. We got somebody or a group of somebodies roving around the middle of the country killing truck drivers. We got a Leeco driver killed in an accident. Within the same general proximity, we got another driver found dead in a rest area. The killer fancies roses and some of the drivers tested positive for drugs. You think we got us a self-proclaimed vigilante?"

Marc moved his hands around on the steering wheel and stretched his arms. "At the very least, yes. I think we have a vigilante trying to even a score for something. The way I see it, there's something seriously unresolved with this person . . . if it's one person. If it's a group, we could be in deep trouble. Not only us, truckers across the country could be in serious jeopardy."

"You think it's got something to do with drugs? I mean, is this person or are these persons on a vendetta for something that's happened in the past or are they on a crusade to scour some more of the residue from the face of the earth? Maybe the trucking industry is just the lucky recipient?"

Marc sighed. "Beats the hell outta me. You know, we thought mandatory drug testing would slow the use of drugs by truckers. Maybe it has . . . a little. The ones who roll eighteen wheels across America's highways and use drugs don't need to be on the road. Public opinion seems to indicate that the truckers who are screaming the loudest are the ones with something to hide. Personally, I don't know the answer. I don't know who's right or who's wrong. I do know that drug usage— from alcohol to cocaine—is destroying this country from the inside out. If we don't do something positive about it very soon . . . well, there may not be anything left for any of us to worry about. I don't know about you, but I'm not going to sit on my butt overdosed with apathy and let that happen."

Carl shifted his weight in the passenger's seat and looked at Marc. "Me neither. No way. I may go down at the end of a blade or in a hail of hellfire, but I ain't gonna die wishing I'd done something about it. I kinda feel that if you ain't part of the solution, then you're a big part of the problem. You think this hitchhiker that Brittin said the trooper checked out has anything to do with all this?"

"He's a shot. Probably a long one, but he's still a shot. Brittin will have the goods on the guy if there are any goods to have. Face it, one hitchhiker stopped by a cop in the vicinity of a crime . . . it certainly narrows the field. Realistically, how many hitchhikers are on the highway in this country at any given moment?"

Carl laughed. "Write your congressman about that one. You could probably get the federal government to spend a few hundred million of the taxpayer's money to do a study."

The familiar Icom speaker interrupted Marc and Carl's conversation with Brittin Crain's blaring voice. "Pathfinder, this is Barnburner. Over."

Marc released the steering wheel with his right hand and reached for the microphone. "This is Pathfinder. Go ahead, Brittin."

"Pathfinder, I got some update on our boy, Donald Puckett. You ready to copy?"

"Roger. Go ahead."

"Let me give you the *Reader's Digest* version first. Donald Puckett—as described by the Arkansas lawman and the Social Security number—doesn't exist. But it doesn't stop there."

———

David Foster eased the Blazer to the side of the road. Behind him, the blue lights flashed on the top of the police car. Bright takedown lights glared into the rear of the Blazer and flooded the interior with hot-white light. The cop positioned his spotlight directly into Foster's outside rearview mirror. Although all of the window glass in the car was tinted two or three shades darker than normal, it couldn't keep the bright lights from the police car from illuminating everything inside, and that worried Foster. He felt his chest pounding, and his heart felt as if it were thrashing rather than beating. Everything inside him screamed a panic alert, but Foster struggled to maintain his composure.

Once the Blazer stopped, it seemed like an eternity before there was any movement behind it. Finally, the silhouette of a man appeared and blotted out the light for an instant. Foster could tell even through the glare in the mirror that the officer was approaching the driver's side of his vehicle. He breathed deeply, kept his hands on the steering wheel, and waited.

When the officer stopped just behind the driver's door, David Foster got a glimpse of his watch in the flood of light that shone from behind him. He was glad he had put it back on his wrist at the truckstop. Even before the lawman spoke, Foster felt a sense of relief and salvation . . . thirty-five seconds until hell came to Russellville, Arkansas. And even in a worst-case scenario, he could fake it that long.

The lawman stayed far enough behind the driver's door that David Foster couldn't see him without turning around in his seat. The man was large and wearing a dark blue uniform. His voice carried across the quiet night air like the bark of a pit bull. "I'd like to see your operator's license, please."

Foster stalled for time. "Uh, did I do something wrong, officer?"

"Just your license, please."

"But why did you stop me? I thought I was driving quite carefully?"

The pit bull barked again. "Nothin' wrong with the

way you're driving. You got a license tag display light out. That's improper equipment."

Foster appeared shocked, but he knew the light was out for a reason. "Damn. I didn't know that. I'll get it repaired first thing in the morning."

"I still need to see your license."

"Is it all right if I get out of the truck. It's kinda hard to get to it in here."

The pit-bull officer barked a command. "Get out slowly and keep your hands where I can see them."

Foster listened and glanced back at his watch. Twenty seconds. "Yes, sir. Whatever you say. I hope you aren't gonna give me a ticket." He opened the driver's door and slid from the seat until he stood on the pavement.

The officer backed away one or two steps and watched every move Foster made. "Now, your license, please."

Foster reached into his hip pocket and came out with his wallet. He found his driver's license and handed it to the officer.

The officer looked at the license carefully and then shined a flashlight into Foster's face. "What are you hauling in the backseat, Mr. Puckett?"

"Computer parts, why?"

"A newspaper route delivery man said you had a companion back at the shopping center. He said the man looked dead. Where is your companion, Mr. Puckett?"

"At the truck, I suppose. What is all this about?"

"Mind if I have a look under that tarp covering your backseat?"

Foster was thankful for the darkness despite the lights from the patrol car. He hoped his fear wasn't showing because on the inside his guts were reeling. "No, not at all. Help yourself. We could even ride back over to the shopping center, and if my friend hasn't driven away, he'll tell you he isn't dead."

The officer's face hardened. "I already did. There's

no one there. Please step away from the vehicle, Mr. Puckett. I do have your consent to search under the tarp?"

Foster nodded affirmatively.

The officer moved toward the Blazer and stuck his head inside. At that instant the ground shook from a massive explosion a mile behind the patrol car. The sky churned with fire towering over everything in view. Above the flames that licked the sky, black smoke funneled into the night. The officer jerked from the Blazer and looked back toward the shopping center. "Holy shit! What was that?"

There was no answer, but the next thing he saw was the man known to him as Donald Puckett holding an automatic pistol, and it was pointed directly at his face. The pit-bull-voiced officer froze and his face etched with fear from something he never thought could happen to him. And it was in that instant that he realized he was going to die.

Foster's bearded face split in a broad smile and his hand held the gun steady. "To answer your question, you'll never know because you already know too much. Bye!"

Chapter Eleven

Marc and Carl digested the information given them by Brittin Crain. The fact that Donald Puckett with the Social Security number given the police dispatcher didn't exist, shed very little new light on the pathway to the killer. It did, however, point a finger of suspicion toward Puckett. But there were other possibilities. First and foremost, the dispatcher could have copied the number incorrectly. Second, the trooper could have misread the number when he gave it to the dispatcher. And third, maybe somewhere along the bureaucratic line somebody messed up and the number was legitimate and the computer data was incorrect. Anything was possible, but Donald Puckett certainly deserved further inquiry.

Marc and Carl had finally reached the scene of Glen Hawthorn's fatal crash. And there, a team of evidence technicians rummaged through the remains of the overroad rig. They had been on the scene for more than two hours, and their task was near completion. But for Marc and Carl, the task had just begun.

The Leeco overroad rig lay on its side, well off the roadway, in a field. Plastic tape and chalk outlines marked the location of Hawthorn's body when the technicians and police arrived on the scene. His body had already been transported to a nearby medical facility for postmortem examination.

Marc had activated the on-board High Definition Television system to record the accident on video tape for future reference. The HDTV system would supply video footage that rivaled the photographic quality of 35 mm color film. While it was doubtful the footage would ever be needed, the Highway Warriors lived by a philosophy that dictated foresight.

Brittin Crain had dispatched one FBI agent to the scene to represent the Bureau's interest in the case and to subtly oversee the investigation.

The Highway Warriors made their entry quietly as representatives of Leeco Freight Lines. Marc had also requested Winston Andrews to roll a bobtail rig toward the crash scene to recover the empty Leeco trailer should it prove roadworthy. That Hawthorn had been deadhead to Dallas from Fort Smith discounted the theory of a possible hijacking for freight. The presence of the dead rose on Hawthorn's body welded him firmly in death to the chain of victims of what would likely prove to be a crazed serial killer. Marc wanted to make sure that the technicians had been thorough, and he also wanted to nose around for anything they might have missed that would prove useful in getting a lead on Glen Hawthorn's murderer.

Marc looked for the FBI agent. When he found him, the fed was packaging evidence gathered by the technicians. "Excuse me, I'm Marc Lee from Leeco Freight Lines. When you get a minute, I'd like to talk with you."

The agent stopped and looked at Marc. He extended his right hand. "I'm Jody Kuiper. I'm the field agent in charge of this little neck of God's country. Agent Crain from Washington told me to expect you. Must be a close friend or something because he threatened my manhood if I didn't extend the full cooperation of the Bureau to you and your friend."

Marc smiled. "He gets excited sometimes."

The agent went back to his work, but he continued the conversation. "Leeco must have some heavy political connections to get Washington interested in anything this time of night . . . anytime, for that matter."

Marc shrugged his shoulders. "I wouldn't know. I just drive a truck occasionally and try to keep the company in the black. Don't have time for much else. You got any idea what happened here?"

Agent Kuiper hesitated. "This for the official record or is it you and me talking?"

"Whichever way I get the most accurate answers."

"Okay, off the record. Somebody iced your driver. Shot him in the face with a twenty-two caliber handgun would be my guess. That caused him to crash. We got some good physical evidence, but good evidence sometimes takes time to analyze. Whoever killed him has long, dark hair. I got some of it from the rear of the passenger's seat and from the doorframe. Judging from the texture, my guess is the killer is a male and he hasn't washed his hair in a while. We'll have to wait for the lab to verify that. Call it my hunch and take it for what it's worth."

Marc nodded his head. "Any indication the Leeco driver was on drugs?"

"Yeah, he was on drugs all right—sinus medication. A no-drowsiness prescription to keep his sinuses clear. Found them in his travel bag. Other than that, we didn't find so much as an aspirin anywhere near the crash scene or inside the rig. The autopsy will tell all of his secrets if there were any. From what I've seen here, I'd say there weren't too many secrets."

Marc nodded his head once more. "Interesting. I appreciate what you're doing here, Mr. Kuiper. On behalf of Leeco Freight Lines, if there is anything we can do to assist your efforts, don't hesitate to ask. I'll make that official or off-the-record assistance. We're anxious to help in any way we can."

Kuiper grinned. "I think I catch the full connotations of that statement. Thanks. I don't know of anything you can do just now. We're in a waiting game until the medical examiner has done his thing and we get the evidence collected here on a plane for the lab. I'd say even if all of us are living right, we're looking at some time tomorrow morning or maybe tomorrow afternoon before we have anything of substance. A killer can cover a lot of ground in that period of time. I wish I had a miracle or a few magic tricks I could slip out of my pocket, but I don't."

Carl grinned as he visually scoured the area.

Marc stood beside him, and a smile creased his face as he spoke. "We all have that feeling once in a while. Real life is usually a little short on miracles."

Kuiper sealed the last evidence envelope and looked up at the Highway Warriors. "I've got to get these packages off to the Bureau's lab. All of this isn't worth anything to us if we don't know what we've got. If you'll forgive me, I'm going to hit the road."

Marc extended his hand for a final handshake of friendship. "Understood. We'll anxiously await your lab's conclusions. I think we'll have a look around before we leave. We have another tractor coming to take the trailer back to Dallas. Thank you for your Bureau's assistance. I hope you find something."

"Me, too," Kuiper quipped, and left the crash scene.

Marc and Carl moved around in the glow of the portable work lights set up around the perimeter of the crash scene. The rig lying dormant in the middle of the giant field reminded Marc of a beached whale abandoned and left to die alone on its side. Whoever was in the rig with Glen Hawthorn when the giant machine crashed would have had to climb for freedom by way of the passenger's door. Moving that door straight up into the air would have been no easy chore, which meant the person had to be in better than average physical condition. It also meant the killer probably wasn't injured. It further meant the perpetrator had to climb to freedom by way of the top, front, or bottom of the rig, since it was lying on the driver's side. If the evidence technicians or the other lawmen at the scene could have missed anything, Marc figured it would be near the bottom of the rig on the ground. The bright white lights lit the crash scene with an efficiency that rivaled daylight. Marc walked around the rig slowly, looking for anything out of place.

Carl strolled leisurely beside him and kicked at the dust beneath their feet. "I know you're fishing for something, but I wouldn't count on finding it. Looks like these people did a very thorough job. Maybe our time would be better spent grabbing some sack time and gettin' ourselves ready for a hard day tomorrow. What say?"

"Yeah, wishful thinking, I'm sure. I guess I want so badly for Glen Hawthorn to be clean. My interests are partially selfish too. I'd like to see him remembered with a clean slate, and I'd certainly like to see Leeco come away without the blemish of a drug-induced fatal crash. We try hard for a clean record. We're a company that works at it. We always have."

"Regardless of which way the autopsy falls, you have to accept it. Leeco is a company of adults who are responsible for their own actions. You can't be there and make critical decisions for them. You hire the best people you can and you impose your company standards. They have to have pride in the company and themselves before they'll play by the rules. It isn't your responsibility."

"Yeah."

"Hey, what's that?"

"What?"

"At the edge of the tire. Something glittered when we stepped past."

Marc strained hard to see what Carl was talking about. "I didn't see it. Where?"

Carl pointed and then knelt down into the dust. He came up with a silvery object not much larger than a big peanut. "This."

Marc took the silvery object and looked carefully.

"It's something wrapped in aluminum foil. Let's take a look." He unwrapped the foil and exposed a yellowish-white caplet inside. He held it out in the palm of his hand and looked at Carl. "I wonder what this is?"

Carl examined the caplet without touching it. "I don't know, but I'll bet you it didn't come from a pharmacy lookin' like that. Not a legal one anyway."

———

The lawman with the pit-bull voice closed his eyes and gritted his teeth in anticipation of the shot that would kill him. It didn't come. Instead, the man known to him as Donald Puckett was spouting orders.

"Get away from my truck now! Hurry!"

The officer responded in his gruff voice. "Okay. Easy with that gun. I'm movin'. Just be easy on that trigger. You don't have to hurt me. I'll manage to forget everything. I swear it!"

"Shut your mouth and move fast." Foster, alias Donald Puckett, waved the Ruger frantically.

"All right, all right. I'm goin'. Please be careful with that gun."

"I said shut your trap. One more word and I'll put a bullet right in your mouth and shut it for you. Move!"

The officer moved slowly and deliberately along the side of the Blazer, his back almost touching it as he stepped sideways. He couldn't see much because of the bright lights from his patrol car behind the truck. What he could see was Puckett holding the gun and not giving an inch. And right now, that was the only thing that mattered.

"Easy, nothing cute or your ass is over. You got that?"

The officer nodded that he understood just as he reached the rear of the Chevy.

"Now, move slowly to your car. The driver's side. When you get there. Get in and keep your hands where I can see them."

The lawman moved carefully, still blinded by the steady white light and the rotating blue lights from the patrol car.

Puckett followed, meticulously inching his way along with the officer. The Ruger was still in his extended right hand, ready.

Halfway between the vehicles, the lawman spun around and threw a wild punch at Foster. The punch missed and a shot rang out. The bullet missed the lawman and slammed harmlessly into the pavement. The officer jumped back and then his right fist thrusted forward and landed with surgical precision on Puckett's left jaw.

Foster was dazed, and out of reactionary panic he fired another wild shot from the Ruger .22 automatic. He stepped back, his conscious mind trying to recoup from the stunning blow.

The officer was undaunted because he knew he was struggling for survival. Even with the threat of gunfire, the pit bull continued the attack. He was on top of Puckett now, wrestling with his gun hand. Foster managed a frantic kick to the lawman's groin. The guy grabbed his testicles and bent over, but only for an instant. Then he was up and swinging like an infuriated pit bull.

Foster took a swing with his left arm and tried to get a line of fire for the Ruger. The punch missed and the Ruger fell to the pavement as a punishing blow into Foster's forearm numbed his fingers for a few seconds. He jerked his arm back and moved upward with a middle block to stop a savage left hook thrown by the struggling cop. His hand was throbbing, his mind in absolute panic. He knew he had to clear his mind and get into his own survival mode, but he couldn't think clearly. His vision faded, then came back again. He felt light-headed, dizzy. And that's when he realized he had a mission . . . for the sake of his family. But in order to accomplish that mission, he had to deal with the cop.

Then he had one fleeting thought—he should have killed the cop the instant he had the drop on him.

The officer had him now, twisting Foster's arm and forcing him to the pavement. His face crashed into the hard surface with a savage ferocity, and he could feel blood trickle from the open wound. And now the lawman was trying to get on top of him. Foster struggled and spun around, his own body weight at least thirty or forty pounds lighter than the big cop's. He managed to make his legs move, and they flew out in a circular arch that caught the lawman just at the back of the knees. The big cop fell beside him on the pavement with a loud thud and a pain-filled groan.

Foster continued the spin and managed to get back to his feet. His military training and instinct took over. He looked for the Ruger, but it was lost somewhere on the pavement. The cop was moving fast now, regaining control of his functions, and his right hand was going for his revolver. Foster moved in with a front kick, and the cop's gun hand flew skyward, but his left came around and caught Foster's leg. Foster lost his balance and fell backward. He threw his left arm out to cushion the impact. He felt intense pain when his body weight settled on the arm, but he managed another roll to the right, and his free foot launched a sweeping kick that landed in the side of the big cop's head.

The lawman rolled sideways, cursing and spitting blood. But he didn't stop. He gathered his momentum and charged Foster while he was still on his hands and knees. He tried for the gun again. Foster stopped the movement with another brutal kick to the head and one to the upper arm. The cop screeched in pain, groaned again, and fell back against the pavement.

Foster moved fast. His eyes searched the pavement for the Ruger, but he still couldn't find it. Then the sound of sirens entered his semiconscious mind. Sirens. More cops? He scrambled toward the cop and kicked him again. The man collapsed on the pavement as he

choked and gasped for air. David Foster didn't back off.
He kicked harder, frustration overpowering his psyche.
When it looked like the cop was finished, Foster kicked
him some more.

The sirens were louder now. He looked over his
shoulder toward the burning overroad rig a mile away at
the strip shopping center. The night sky was glowing red
from the burning vehicle, and flames licked into the
blackened darkness that shrouded Russellville, Arkansas. That's when he realized the sirens weren't coming to
help the cop, they were headed toward the fire.

Foster turned his attention to the Ruger. He had to
find the Ruger, and then he had to get as much distance
between himself and the cop as he could before someone
missed the pudgy old lawman. He looked hard for the
weapon. Then he saw a reflection in the street just
beyond the glare of the takedown lights on the patrol car.
He staggered toward the reflection.

The Ruger.

Foster bent forward to retrieve the gun and as his
fingers wrapped around the pistol's grips, thunder
roared behind him.

The cop.

Foster fell to the pavement and rolled right. The
Ruger came up in his hands and his eyes searched for
the target. His head throbbed from a combination of the
beating he had taken from the cop and the frightening
roar of the lawman's weapon behind him. His sight was
blinded from the patrol car's floodlights. With his head
screaming every alarm it knew, Foster leveled the
Ruger's sights on the pit-bull cop who was half-sitting,
half-lying on the pavement.

Foster worked the Ruger's trigger three times in
rapid succession. The pit-bull lawman's body slumped,
twitched, and then collapsed. David Foster fumbled to
his knees and then got to his feet. He moved to the cop
and knelt beside him. One shot missed, but two scored
dead ringers in the man's forehead. Foster kicked the

cop's gun from dead fingers to the side of the street. He moved as fast as his aching body could until he reached the open door of the Blazer. He climbed back inside and started the engine. He hurt all over, but somehow he managed to get the Blazer into gear. His foot slammed the accelerator to the floor and the Blazer lurched forward. Behind him, the patrol car sat idle with its emergency lights still flashing and the body of the lawman sprawled on the street in front of it.

David Foster traveled north on Arkansas Route 7 for twenty-five minutes. He wiped the dried and drying blood from his nose and face, the result of the officer slamming him into the pavement. He tried to gather himself. He talked aloud to himself in an effort to convince himself that the crazy cop had it coming. Still, he wasn't sure. At the edge of the Ozark National Forest on Route 7, Foster had a traumatic thought that caused his heart to sink: the cop still had his driver's license.

———

At the strip shopping center the fire from Larry Cummings's rig raged out of control. Fire units from the little town of Russellville battled the blazing inferno with patient diligence. Two police cars sat away from the fire units and watched the flames consume the massive overroad rig. And at the edge of the shopping center buildings, a young man watched the show from the comfort of his pickup truck. He watched for fifteen minutes until he decided to go talk with one of the patrolmen standing beside a police car. The young pickup driver got out and walked to the patrol car.

"Mother sure is blazing, ain't it?"

The officer had little to say at first. His only response was, "Yeah."

"I knew that guy was up to something when he got out of this truck. I didn't think about him burnin' it."

That caught the cop's attention. "You mean you saw something here?"

"Sure did. I'm the one that called. I flagged down one of your men and he stopped the fellow a mile or so out the road. Didn't you hear that on your radio or something?"

"I heard Alvin Shepard make a traffic stop, that's all. What did you see here?"

"I saw the guy park the truck and get out. He opened up a Chevrolet Blazer that sat here for a day or two and then he took the other guy out and stuffed him in the backseat. I think the other guy was dead, I swear I do. He sure as hell wasn't movin' and this fellow had to haul him over his shoulder. I even talked to the rascal. I knew something wasn't just right with him. I could feel it."

The officer had produced a notebook, and he worked feverishly to gather notes on everything the man said. "What's your name?"

"Billy Kershaw. I deliver the morning newspapers on this side of town. Hell, I seen it all. I seen him put something in the fuel tanks too. That's what made this baby cook."

"Okay, Billy, I'm Dean Carlisle. I want you to go over this real slow, but wait just a moment until I call Alvin on the radio and we'll get him over here."

Carlisle opened his patrol car door and grabbed the microphone. He made a call three times for Officer Alvin Shepard, but he didn't get an answer. After the third unanswered call, he called the dispatcher. "Yeah, Howard. Where'd Alvin go after he made that traffic stop thirty or forty-five minutes ago."

Howard, the dispatcher, answered. "Just a minute and I'll look. He should be on the air. Well, now, let's see. No, I don't show him signing back on in the log, but I know he did. Uh, at least I think he did. He called in the tag, yeah, here it is. An Arkansas tag on a Chevy Blazer about a mile from the shopping center where you boys got that fire."

Carlisle looked at Billy Kershaw. "Hop in if you

want to take a little ride. Let's go be sure Alvin made that stop all right."

Kershaw excitedly leaped at the opportunity. "Hot damn!" He ran to the patrol car and got in. "I knew something wasn't right when I seen that passenger lookin' so dead. Hot damn, I knew it. Damn good thing I got a good look at the fellow, huh?"

"Yeah, damn good thing," Carlisle said as he pressed the accelerator to the floor heading for Officer Alvin Shepard's last known location.

Chapter Twelve

David Foster decided the best thing to do was accept his screw-up and keep moving. The further he could separate himself from the melee in Russellville, the better. Once he had taken time to think about it, the fact that the pit-bull cop had retained his driver's license was more an inconvenience than a threat. After all, Donald J. Puckett had been dead for years and the Social Security number was a fake. Sure, the description on the license matched, but the photo was taken with long hair and a beard. That wasn't a big deal, at least nothing a few minutes with some scissors and a razor couldn't remedy. The worst that could happen, he figured, was that he would be stopped again and get a ticket for not having a driver's license. But now the mission was more important—Larry Cummings had to get what was coming to him for the senseless killing of the entire Foster family. Truckers on drugs had to get a message that the needless murder and mayhem on America's highways had to stop.

Foster relied on the fact that by the time anyone could unweave the web he had meticulously woven to disguise his true identity, his mission would be accomplished and he would set off for another base camp on another mountain. And he had decided that people driving trucks or even cars had to get his message clearly. When he was finished with Larry Cummings, he would go back to the road until he had done all he could to rid the world of selfish, inconsiderate druggies. When the word got out that there was more for the druggies to fear than the police, Foster even thought he might become a hero for the decent people who didn't believe in synthetic strength and courage.

Such thoughts helped ease the pain Foster felt from not only his domestic loss, but the beating he had taken from the big cop. He turned the Blazer onto the dirt logging road that threaded its way through the Ozark Mountains to his 4 X 4 ATV. Morning would be coming across the eastern horizon soon, but now the night was deep black and dotted by a heaven full of stars.

In the backseat Larry Cummings slept in a drug-induced trance. When he awakened, he would find himself surrounded by a brutal and foreign forest so dense that a man could get lost there and never find his way out again. That forest was a refuge for David Foster, but it would soon become a living hell for Larry Cummings.

It was quite difficult for Foster to find the secluded hideaway he had constructed for the ATV. The dark, dense forest, illuminated only by headlights from the Blazer, looked all the same from the windshield. Had it not been for his forethought, Foster could easily have missed it. But he had planned ahead for every possibility he could imagine when he built his reclusive retreat high in the mountains and that included markings recognizable only to him. He found them and drove the Blazer directly to his camouflaged shelter.

Foster used the light from the Blazer's headlights to illuminate the area covered in brush and camouflage netting that shielded the ATV. He finally cleared all of the brush and fired the 4 X 4 off-road machine. He had, several months earlier, built a makeshift litter from young trees cut in the forest. The combination litter and sled had seen much use in the transfer of materials to and from the site of the retreat high in the mountains. This would be the first time he had ever carried a person on it, but the rig would work equally well for that purpose also. Foster attached the litter to the back of the

ATV and double-checked to see that it was secure. When he was ready to roll, he gathered his backpack and slung the straps over his shoulders. He returned to the Blazer and pulled the tarp off of Larry Cummings. The big trucker still slept peacefully in the backseat. Foster managed to sit the sleeping man up in the seat, and then he lifted him out of the Blazer.

Cummings was heavy and his dead weight caused Foster to strain when he dragged the man by the shoulders to the litter. Once he had the sleeping trucker on the litter, he strapped him in place with flexible rubber tie-down cords. Foster double-checked all of his work, locked the Blazer, and mounted the ATV 4 X 4 for the long ride to his hidden retreat at the top of the mountain.

The pathway that led high into the mountains was extremely hazardous. Most of the route was the remnants of logging trails used many years before when the U.S. Forest Service sold timber rights to the highest bidders as a part of their wildlife and forest conservation and development program. Accessibility to the leaf-covered, rut-filled tentacles that etched through the ridges and valleys of the high mountain forest was limited to ATVs or helicopters. Years of erosion had etched away any portion of the logging roads that could be traveled by the best street machines. Foster's two years in the mountains had carved a permanent map in his mind. Natural landmarks, some hardly more than broken limbs or a rotting stump, lined the trail back to the cabin. As the ATV wove its way through the high country, Foster had another awakening similar to the one when he'd driven the Blazer through the forest— everything looked the same in the artificial light of the ATV's headlights. That, coupled with a high level of nervousness now made travel slow and delicate.

Foster trudged forward, inching his way against the darkness and hoping for the first glittering fingers of light that would soon split the dark horizon. With that light would come the ability to navigate through the dense woodlands. Near the top of the mountain were explosive devices with pressure triggers that would present a deadly challenge even in daylight. Foster knew the shroud of darkness would mask the devices even more, and running through the maze would be extremely risky. There was only one narrow opening in the perimeter around the cabin that was free of explosives, and that opening was only one foot wider than the wheel base of the Honda ATV. To find the inlet in the dark would present a very difficult challenge, one that permitted no margin for error. Even if he could spot the clear inlet, a six inch error in either direction and both he and Larry Cummings would be hamburger.

Foster neared a sharp rock precipice that spanned a deep washout in the pathway. The rock, more than ten feet across and an apparent result of a heavy rainfall in years past, had slid into the roadway and formed a natural bridge. Below the large flat rock was more darkness. Foster knew from previous inspections that the washout had cut a gorge at least fifty feet deep, and it was lined with jutting rocks from top to bottom. The rain had fallen with such ferocity that the area below the logging road had become a massive mud slide. Over the years since the rain, only minor vegetation had grown in the deep dried mud. It had, however, been sufficient to keep the forces of nature from further eroding the otherwise wooded landscape.

Foster approached the giant rock with cautious apprehension. His previous examinations of the natural bridge had proven the precarious nature of the giant rock's final resting place. Soil supporting the bridge was dangerously loosened from the onslaught of the rain that created the abyss in the first place. Although the weight of the four-wheeler was unlikely to break the rock free, anything was possible in the limitless boundaries of nature. Should the boulder break free of its support structure, Foster knew his dedicated mission in life would be both complete and over in the same tragic plunge. If another route to the cabin existed, he would have surely used it, but it didn't. That meant cross the rock or leave the ATV behind and walk the remaining distance to the cabin.

He inched forward. The front wheels of the machine moved onto the rock. Foster gave the machine a little more gas and let it slip slowly onto the boulder. Behind him, the scraping sounds of the sled against the rock caught his attention. He looked back and studied the outline of the wooden structure in the backlight of the headlights. All clear. He kept moving until the front wheels of the ATV cleared the bridge.

That's when it happened.

The scraping grew louder from the sled and something was wrong. Foster looked back again. The sled was pivoting and sliding toward the edge of the precipice. Foster tried to gun the engine, but the sudden lurch caused the ATV to shift sideways. Now the sled was at the edge and Larry Cummings was sleeping at the threshold of death's door without even knowing it.

Foster panicked. His heart raced and felt as if it would jump from his chest. He hit the throttle and the ATV lurched sideways. The sled was over the edge now, dangling in free space above the washout gorge below. Cummings's dead weight was pulling, causing the ATV's engine to whine and the rubber tires to lose their grip on the smooth, dew-dampened rock. The engine roared now, and the sled pulled the ATV to the edge. There was only a foot to go before both the ATV and the sled plummeted into the deadly darkness below. Larry Cummings's tranquilized body hung freely over the edge now, and the only thing between him and death was the four rubber tie-down straps. In the backlight Foster could see the knot that attached the sled to the ATV start to slip and fray from the extreme tension.

It was a final effort. Foster opened the throttle as far as it would go. The machine bucked and groaned against the harsh opposing force. The rear tires threw black smoke from their effort to gain traction on the moist rock, and the front tires uselessly clawed into leaf-covered soil. Foster felt the machine move, and he looked to the rear at the sled just as the right rear ATV tire lost its grip with the rock and slipped over the edge.

David Foster screamed into the pitch-black darkness.

———

Brittin Crain had decided to try something different. When the information of the state trooper's inquiry on the hitchhiker Donald Puckett came to light, Crain decided to red flag the name, Social Security number, and date of birth for Donald J. Puckett. Although driver's license information requested from the various states and accumulated into NCIC showed more than seventy-four Donald J. Pucketts, only one had the date of birth logged by the Arkansas state police dispatcher. Granted, it was a long shot, but he had taken longer ones and come out on top. The fact that the hitchhiker had been in the general vicinity of the rest area at or near the approximate time of death for the truck driver found there was too substantial to overlook. Sure, it was a hunch, but it was also too relevant to toss aside without further consideration.

Once Crain had red-flagged the name and information in the NCIC computer, any law enforcement agency with access to the criminal information computer network that entered Puckett's name would find the alert. Crain's purpose was two fold. First, he simply wanted to see if Donald J. Puckett showed up anywhere else through any other law enforcement agency. And second, he wanted to be notified personally of any inquiries. If Donald J. Puckett aroused the curiosity of any police officer in the United States, Brittin Crain would get an alert call via NCIC.

Crain realized Puckett was probably a man on the

run from something since his Social Security number had proven to be an imposter. That fact alone didn't make Puckett a prime murder suspect. It did, on the other hand, make the name and the man worthy of further investigation. Puckett showed no NCIC criminal history, which simply meant he had never been arrested.

Brittin ran every conceivable combination of inquiries, and still the computer came out with nothing. When he finished with NCIC, Crain entered military files in search of a military history. There was none. That done, he inquired into the federal data base holding all selective service registrants for the past thirty years. Still, no Donald J. Puckett with any date of birth or physical description that even remotely resembled the information given by the state trooper to his dispatcher. That meant one of two things: Donald J. Puckett didn't exist or he had lived in a closet all of his life. And for a man professing to be in his midthirties, that wasn't very likely.

Every avenue Brittin approached became a dead-end street. He glanced at the clock and realized the night had gotten completely away from him. It was four-thirty in the morning, and he could do little until much later in the day. He picked up the telephone and rang the control operator in communications two floors below him in the Justice Department building.

A sleepy voice answered. "Kirkwood."

Crain's voice was just as sleepy. "Tommy, this is Crain. I'm going back to the dispensary and make an attempt to grab some shut-eye. I've entered some NCIC red flags. If we get a hit or if I get activity on F-twelve, wake me. I'll keep the phone by my head, but let the sucker ring if I don't grab it right away."

"Long night, huh?"

"Yeah, a long one. You sound like you could use some sleep yourself. You gonna make it?"

"Hey, I always make it. Well, I have to admit some

nights are better than others. This is one of the others."

"What's her name?"

"Kathy. You're perceptive for a man with no sleep."

Crain laughed. "No big thing. I chase 'em myself when I can get away from here."

"One thing. Agent Crain. I have no audio connection to F-twelve. Just an indicator light. It's a priority frequency that requires special clearance. Nobody's seen fit for the poor humble dispatcher to have access to it. If it pops up busy, you want me to call you so you can answer it?"

"Yeah, you got it. I'm headin' for the sack. See you."

"Right. Sweet dreams."

Brittin laid the telephone down and stood from the computer desk. He stretched hard, took a few deep breaths, and headed for the door. Without a look back, Crain switched the lights off in his private office and walked to the dispensary down the hallway. He had decided it would be easier to sleep there than to take the thirty-minute drive home. The bunk was halfway comfortable and the sheets were clean. Once he fluffed the pillow, it would be like home.

Crain's head had hardly hit the freshly fluffed pillow when the telephone rang. He struggled to open his eyes and scramble for the source of the sound. "Yeah?"

Kirkwood's voice was awake and alert. "Sorry to wake you, Heavy Eyes, but I got a hit on an NCIC red flag. A subject by the name of Puckett, Donald J."

"Where?"

"A little town in Arkansas named Russellville. Your boy Puckett killed one of their finest a couple of hours ago. Left 'em quite a mess from what I hear. I made a phone call for verification as soon as I got the hit. He's sure got 'em stirred up out there."

"Well, are they sure? Is he in custody?"

"Yeah, they're sure and no, he isn't in custody. He got away. The police chief of Russellville is waiting on your call."

"If he got away, how do they know it was Donald J. Puckett?"

Kirkwood laughed. "Your boy screwed up. The dead cop still had his driver's license from a traffic stop."

"No shit?"

"It's too late at night or too early in the morning for bad jokes, Crain. There's one more thing."

"Okay, shoot."

"According to Russellville's chief, Puckett killed or kidnapped a truck driver and torched his rig. The driver hasn't been found and Puckett's long gone."

———

One of the many luxuries of the Leeco high-tech overroad rig was the comfortable sleeper. The Highway Warriors were taking advantage of it. They had decided that little or nothing could be accomplished until lab reports came in from the FBI. The killer or killers had been thorough and there was nothing concrete to go on that would lead them to the culprit. Frustration aside, it had been a long, tiresome day, so Marc and Carl decided to rest while there was still time.

They had left the crash scene where Glen Hawthorn lost his life. The yellowish-white caplet found there had been sealed in a plastic container for shipment to Brittin Crain for analysis, but that couldn't be accomplished until daylight. The Warriors drove to Fort Smith and parked the rig there.

The closest thing to a lead in the case was the new input on the hitchhiker named Puckett. The Highway Warriors had discussed the issue and decided to get to the Fort Smith area and cautiously talk with the state trooper who had stopped Puckett.

Once the rig was parked and the sleeper prepared, sleep had come easily for the Warriors. The last twenty-four hours had been stressful, and they were ready to put all of the events behind them. The encounter with the drug traffickers on the interstate and then the death of one of Leeco's own had taken its toll. Although both men were conditioned to long periods without sleep, logic and their bodies demanded that they rest.

They had been asleep for only two hours when the one-kilohertz paging tone blared from the Icom's speaker. Immediately following the tone, Brittin Crain's excited voice came from the radio receiver via the Defense Department ComSat-D satellite link.

"Pathfinder, this is Barnburner. Do you copy?"

Marc sat upright in the sleeper and shook his head. "The man has no mercy," he said sleepily.

Carl rolled over and rubbed his eyes. "What's the saying? Something about no rest for the weary?"

Crain's voice blarred again. "Pathfinder, this is Barnburner. Urgent traffic, do you copy?"

Carl sat up. "You want to get it or do you want me to?"

Marc moved to the front of the sleeper toward the passenger area inside the Leeco cab. "Stay comfortable. I'll get it."

Carl laid down again and stretched. "No argument from me."

Marc made it into the front of the cab and picked up the microphone. "Barnburner, this is Pathfinder. You have traffic?"

Crain replied. "Top of the morning to you. Were you sleeping?"

"Yeah."

"Short and concise. I like that. Well, I was too, but we got something."

Marc keyed the transmitter. "I'm listening."

"I think we got our boy. Last known location was Russellville, Arkansas, and I believe his lead is shrinking."

The squelch tail sounded and Marc answered. "I'm still listening."

"Okay, listen carefully. An hour or two ago, a cop in

Russellville made a traffic stop. He called in the license plate number of the vehicle he was stopping. During that same time frame, an explosion occurred nearby and the dispatcher had his attention diverted to that. He forgot about the cop and the traffic stop. When they finally got to him, he'd been shot in the face with what appeared to be a twenty-two. He still had the driver's license of the man he'd stopped when they found him. That license belonged to Donald J. Puckett. Over."

"Okay, so it points to Puckett. What does it prove about involvement in what we're working on? I thought this Puckett was hitchhiking."

The radio was silent for several seconds and then Brittin responded. "Okay, stay with me a minute. You're right, but here's the clincher. Puckett doesn't really exist . . . that is as Donald J. Puckett. The explosion . . . an eighteen-wheeler. The occupant of the truck . . . wanna guess?"

Marc didn't hesitate. "Puckett?"

"You got it."

Marc waited before he answered. "How do you know it was Puckett?"

"The best way there is . . . an eyewitness. A newspaper delivery boy saw him and talked to him. He saw another man with him in the cab of the rig, and Puckett told him the guy was sleeping. Anyway, this kid watched Puckett move the sleeping or dead or whatever-he-was man from the rig to a Chevrolet Blazer. The kid called the cops and that's why the traffic stop. Then the rig blew and the explosion shifted all the attention to the burning rig that was parked in a shopping center parking lot. Over."

Marc digested everything Brittin was saying and something didn't fit. "If it was Puckett and Puckett, per se, doesn't exist, then who is the guy or do you know?"

After the squelch tail, Crain answered. "It took

some fancy finger work on the old federal keyboard, but I think I've nailed him down. I ran the license plate number the cop called in. It was registered to Puckett at a phony address. This guy has covered his tracks well, but there was a slip. I took the vehicle identification number from the registration and ran it for a history through Arkansas. The Blazer was titled in Arkansas on a transferred title from Ohio. The vehicle was purchased new in Ohio a little over two years ago. The original purchaser was a guy named David Foster, and he made a sale transfer to Donald J. Puckett. Are you with me?"

Marc replied immediately. "Roger. Tell me more."

"All right. I ran a history of David Foster through Ohio and found something real interesting. His driver's license expired last year and it was never renewed. The physical description on the Ohio DL info fits our boy Puckett to the letter . . . sans the long hair and beard. I did a phone check to the PD in a little suburban town just outside of Dayton, and that's when I hit the motherlode."

Marc was fully awake now. He responded immediately. "Don't keep me in suspense."

Brittin continued. "A little more than two years ago, Foster's entire family was killed in a crash on an interstate highway. They were burned beyond recognition when an eighteen-wheeler hit them from behind. The driver was convicted, served fifteen-months, and walked. He was confirmed to be on drugs when the crash occurred. Shortly after that, Foster sold his house, bought the Blazer, and disappeared from the face of the earth. The driver of the rig that killed Foster's family was a man named Larry Cummings. I've just, within the last five minutes, confirmed that Larry Cummings was the driver of the rig that exploded in Russellville. He was on his way to Chicago with a load, but somehow, David Foster, AKA Donald J. Puckett, found him. I figure he plans to take him out, and I also figure he has a place somewhere in the vicinity of Russellville. There's a range of mountains north of there where a man could disappear for a long time. We've got the motive and the background, now all we need is David Foster. And that's your job."

Chapter Thirteen

David Foster's scream echoed through the darkness, but it didn't stop the ATV from sliding toward the edge of the rock bridge. Larry Cummings was totally suspended in free space over the dark edge now, the **rubber** tie-downs stretching from the strain of his weight. His only umbilical cord to life was a small hank of rope tied to the ATV.

Foster had to make an immediate decision—jump and lose both the focus of his vengeance and his transportation, or make the machine go forward.

He let off the throttle until the tires stopped spinning. The ATV stopped, groaned, and then skidded another inch toward certain death. Then it stopped completely. Foster squeezed the hand brakes and held tightly to the handle bars. He sat that way for what seemed like an eternity, but it was only seconds. He looked back at the litter and Larry Cummings, and then he craned his neck to inspect the rope that held the litter. His hands sweated from the intense tension, and he could also feel his chest chilling from perspiration.

The ATV was solid, and Cummings appeared to be in no immediate danger unless the machine moved closer to the edge of the rock. Foster lifted his hand off of the right handle bar and immediately switched the ATV's ignition off. The engine faded and died. Slowly, Foster climbed from the seat. He moved cautiously, testing the result of each movement before he committed himself to it. The ATV groaned again, this time from the strain of Larry Cummings's dead weight pulling it into the dark hole and from the shift of weight realized when Foster moved.

It held steady.

Foster slipped off of the machine and stood on the rock bridge. He moved slowly to the secure edge of the bridge at the front of the ATV. He assessed the problem as best he could in the light of his mini-MagLite. The tires on the 4 X 4 machine seemed to be losing traction because the rock was covered in dew. At the front, the tires clawed into the loose dirt, and there was nothing solid for them to grip.

"No sweat," Foster said aloud. He moved away from the ATV and found several pieces of deadfall limbs using the mini-Mag to scour the forest floor. He broke the limbs into sections two feet long and laid them beneath the front tires, so that when he applied some power, the limbs would slip under the rubber. When he was satisfied enough sticks had been laid, he found a larger limb and cleared away the layer of dew-moistened leaves. He dropped to his knees and started digging in the rich soil. In minutes he had a pile of dirt almost a foot high lying beside his knees. He moved it one double-handful at a time to the rock at the rear ATV tires. He laid enough dirt to cover the wet rock, and then he gathered small twigs to place on top of the dirt.

The trail was paved for survival and the final realization of his innermost hatred.

Foster climbed slowly back on board the ATV and started the engine. He dropped the machine into the lowest gear and eased off the clutch. The ATV engine rumbled and the vehicle moved slightly forward. Then it started to spin, but the sticks and dirt caught beneath the tires and the machine held traction.

Foster gave it a little gas, not too much, but just enough to get it to move. Behind him, the litter scraped against the hard rock. Pieces of wood dislodged and fell into the darkness, but Larry Cummings was unscathed.

Three feet to go.

Foster slowly and deliberately gave the machine more gas. He turned around to check the litter again. Slowly, very slowly, it moved toward the flat area atop the rock bridge.

Two feet remaining.

The front tires were catching good now, the stick sections providing the necessary footing. At the rear, traction was holding. The litter was perched like a see-saw on the edge of the rock. Larry Cummings was still sleeping soundly from the overdose of drugs and oblivious to his near-fatal plunge.

One foot to safety.

The front tires slipped and threw a stick against the undercarriage of the machine. Foster grabbed the brakes, depressed the clutch, and let off the throttle. He inspected everything, took a deep breath, and let the clutch out slowly one more time. The machine moved easier this time, the rear tires pulling where the front ones slipped.

Six inches and he had made it.

Foster turned around to check the litter. He wasn't about to lose his prize catch now. The ATV moved methodically and then he reached safety. Clear.

The rear tires came back on the sticks and the leaf-covered ground of the forest floor. The litter cleared the lethal edge of the rock and steadied on the forest floor behind the ATV. David Foster breathed a sigh of relief. He stopped and inspected the rope and the tie-downs holding Cummings. Everything was secure so he mounted the ATV and continued along the logging road toward his cabin.

The first glittering, golden rods of morning sunlight pierced the sky when Foster stopped the ATV in front of his hand-built cabin. He checked Cummings again to verify his sleeping condition. Satisfied, he went inside the cabin to make a fast security check.

One quick glance at the inside of his reclusive home and he knew that neither man nor beast had violated his sanctity in his absence. But then, intrusion in such an isolated place would have to come more by accident than by predetermined effort.

Foster went back outside and walked to a large cage he had constructed near the cabin. He had seen such structures used by the North Vietnamese Regulars and the Viet Cong on news reports of the war. They had served their purpose well there, so he had decided to construct one for his own use.

The cage was assembled from young hickory and oak saplings, because of their hardness and strength. It stood six feet tall and measured slightly over four feet square. The sections of wood were bound together by vines, rope, and wire. The upright sections of wood were spaced at about three-inch intervals. Its construction, like everything else Foster had built, was exceptionally rigid. Had the occasion arisen, he wouldn't have been hesitant to place a captive full-grown bear in it. Foster smiled with pleasure because it would certainly hold Larry Cummings, especially since the man's physical condition would soon be on a course of rampant deterioration.

Foster returned to the litter and Larry Cummings. He unsnapped the heavy black rubber tie-downs and lifted Cummings to his shoulder. For the second time the man's dead weight surprised him, but Foster managed to get the trucker to the cage. He lowered him into the cage and dropped him onto the floor. Before Foster left Cummings there, he took everything from his pockets. When that was finished, he shut the cage door and secured it with a section of logging chain and a heavy padlock.

From Foster's best estimates, it would be another four to six hours before Cummings regained consciousness. That would be plenty of time to rest and then contemplate the preparations for his own version of hell.

Larry Cummings's hell.

———

Marc Lee and Carl Browne watched the first glimmering rays of morning sun penetrate the sky over the top of Larry Cummings's charred eighteen-wheeler rig in Russellville, Arkansas. Whatever the cause of the fire, the arsonist's work had been undeniably effective. The once bold and stately overroad rig was now a heap of smouldering rubble. Everything, including any physical evidence that might have been present, had been destroyed. The fire had been so hot that even the pavement on which the rig sat had bubbled into a molten mixture of tar and gravel. Two fire engines and several police cars remained on the scene, but the high level of excitement that the fire had first generated had dwindled to cautious guardianship.

Marc had parked the Leeco overroad rig at the end of the parking lot as far away from the remaining action as they could. Both men were tired from lack of sleep but anxious to learn anything that might point them in the direction of David Foster.

The body of the slain police officer had long since been removed and the highway cleared of everything except a bitter memory of the incident. David Foster, alias Donald J. Puckett, had covered his tracks painstakingly and efficiently. He had, once again, managed to disappear without so much as a logical trace. But in his haste, he had committed one serious mistake . . . the driver's license. And although Donald J. Puckett didn't really exist, Brittin Crain's astute criminal mind and the federal government's highly efficient computer system had capitalized on Foster's error. The result was a complete disclosure of the man's true identity. But unfortunately, knowing *who* he was and knowing *where* he was were two totally different animals.

Carl surveyed the arson handiwork. "This guy's a good torch. He didn't leave much."

Marc looked at the smoking truck skeleton and

shook his head. "I wonder if this is a sample of what he's going to do to the guy who was driving this thing. If it is, the bastard's in for a very hard time."

Carl nodded. "What do you think Foster's plan is? You think he's stalked this Cummings guy or was it a stroke of luck on Foster's part?"

"Who knows? Foster is out to avenge the death of his family from the information that's coming together. With no more than we have to go on, he just might make it before anyone can stop him. This is a big country. He could be anywhere by now."

Carl's face filled with seriousness. "Are you convinced it's Foster?"

"I've known Brittin Crain a lot of years. In all that time, I've never seen the man jump to a conclusion. If he says it's Foster, you can bet your balls it's Foster. Brittin runs down everything until the leads run dry or he has solid evidence. To answer your question, yeah, it's Foster all right."

"Where do we go from here?"

"Nowhere until we have some of the lab evidence from autopsies and chemical analyses. My money still says Glen Hawthorn was straight and clean. If I'm right, Foster has needlessly killed an innocent man. I just wonder how many more innocents have died because of him?"

Carl had no answer.

Marc walked around the ruins well out of the way of the remaining firemen. "Another thing bothers me. Foster killed that cop and Brittin said there was an eyewitness to Foster moving Cummings or at least Cummings's body from the rig to another vehicle. I'd like to talk to that witness."

"We gotta tread lightly. We're truck drivers, remember?"

Marc forced a smile. "Yeah, I know. Problem is, if Foster has taken to killing cops, he'll kill anyone who gets in his way. He's out there somewhere and he's volatile. I'd like to nail him before he kills more innocent people."

Carl's face hardened. "What's your feeling on Cummings?"

"What do you mean?"

"You think he's just getting what he's got coming to him?"

"According to Brittin, Cummings served his time. He's had his punishment. Now granted, fifteen months isn't much for killing a family while you're high on drugs and driving a big truck. My feeling is, the system has done its thing and it's none of our concern. What Foster doesn't understand is he's fighting the fire by trying to extinguish the top of the flame. You've got to go deeper. Go for the dealers and the importers. This country doesn't have enough caskets to bury all of the users. Take away the fuel and the fire dies out. All Foster has done is bring himself down to his enemy's level and made himself a wanted man."

"Isn't that kinda what you and me did a while back?"

Marc stopped walking and looked at Carl. "No! What we did was go after the scourge once we knew who they were and what they had done. We have never killed anybody that didn't need killing. And you know something? Even at that, I don't like the killing. I never have. I only do what has to be done. Somebody's got to stop the criminal rampage in this country and that's what the president hired us to do. Sure, we've broken some rules and thrown most of 'em away, but the criminal fire is burning out of control and the damned system isn't doing anything to stop it. The president is."

Carl took it in stride. "You think Foster is wrong? You think he's different from us?"

"Yeah, he's wrong. Dead wrong. And he's different because me and you have never taken the life of an innocent man. Not even once. And you know something else?"

"What's that?"

Marc took a deep breath and looked into Carl's dark brown eyes. "The day either one of us does that—takes an innocent life—I'm out of this forever."

Carl put his hands in his pockets and started walking again. "Yeah, me too."

"I'm doing what I believe in. I'm doing it because I think it's right and I think the real majority of society thinks it's right. I'll spread my own brand of cleansing fire until I see the scum on its knees or I'm dead. But there's nothing that could make me kill an innocent man. Nothing."

Carl examined the torched rig thoroughly. "Yeah, the criminals are doing a damned efficient job of that without any help. Damned efficient."

Marc moved in the direction of three police officers huddled together. "Let's go see if we can find this eyewitness."

Carl followed in stride. "I'm with you, Colonel."

They reached the police congregation and Marc spoke first. "Hi, guys. I'm Marc Lee and this is Carl Browne. We work for Leeco Freight Lines out of Dallas. We're doing some follow-up work on a case that involved the death of one of our drivers south of here. We have reason to believe the guy that did this—this Puckett fellow—we believe he may have had something to do with our driver's death."

One of the officers spoke. "I'm Chief Miller. What is it you wanna know?"

"Well, we've been told there was an eyewitness to at least some of Puckett's handiwork. We'd like to talk to him and get some physical information on the guy. Is that possible?"

Miller was hesitant, but then he mellowed. "Well, I don't like to do that sort of thing with civilians, but I guess since this one is maybe touchin' a lot of people it won't do no harm. That's him sittin' over there in that pickup truck." Chief Miller pointed to a white pickup truck across the paved lot. "He hasn't left here since all this started in the middle of the night last night. The boy's name is Billy Kershaw. Damned nice kid too. I know his daddy right well. Talk to him if you think it'll help you. And good luck."

Marc extended his hand to Chief Miller. "Thanks, Chief. I hope you get this case resolved."

Miller forced a sarcastic smile as he shook Marc's hand. "Don't worry. Puckett will get what he's got coming. If we don't get him, somebody will. Bet your ass on that. Somebody will."

———

Billy Kershaw had witnessed more excitement in the past few hours than he had seen in his entire life before he spotted Donald Puckett. He was getting sleepy, but when he saw two men walking in his direction he snapped wide awake.

When the men stopped beside his open window, he smiled. "Howdy, fellows. I don't think I've seen you in these parts before. I'm Billy Kershaw."

Marc shook hands with Kershaw. "I'm Marc Lee and this is Carl Browne. We work for Leeco Freight Lines out of Dallas, and Chief Miller said you saw all of what happened here last night. Mind if we ask you a few questions?"

Billy smiled and opened the pickup truck door. He stepped out and stood beside the two giant men. Suddenly he felt refreshed because someone was finally paying some attention to what he had to say. "Yeah, I seen it all. Well, most of it. Whatta you wanna know?"

Carl grinned. "Just tell us what you saw."

"Well, I was delivering my papers to the customers here in the strip. I'd seen that Chevy Blazer parked here for a couple of days and there wasn't no one around it. Well, anyway, when I came back this big truck was parked here and a man was movin' around outside it. I watched for a couple minutes and I seen this man go into the Blazer. I drove over to him and talked to him a minute. I even give him a paper. I seen this other man asleep or dead or something in the big truck. Well, I left and got myself in a good position to see what was goin' on. This man I talked to, Puckett, well he took this other man out and carried him on his shoulder to the Blazer and put him in the backseat. I watched him cover him over with a blue tarp. That's when I left and went to get Alvin Shepard over at the doughnut shop a block over. He was gettin' himself some coffee and such. Well, when I got back, the Blazer was gone. Alvin followed the rascal and stopped him a mile or so out the road. That's when all hell blew up back over here. Damn fire flew a hundred feet into the sky, I'm telling you."

Marc looked stunned. "Did you tell all this to the police?"

Billy laughed. "I sure as hell did, but old Chief Miller don't take me none too seriously. He knows my dad and all. He says I'm full of a bunch of hair-brained stuff. But I'll tell you, mister. I know damn well what I saw."

Marc thought everything over carefully. "You said you talked to him. What did he have to say?"

"Oh, nothing much. He wasn't too talkative. Looked like I scared the piss out of him if you want to know the truth. Like I caught him at somethin', which I guess I did. Hell, if I'd a known he was a killer, I'd stayed away from him 'stead of tryin' to make conversation with him."

Carl responded quickly. "What do you mean when you say he looked like you'd caught him at something?"

Billy leaned against the side of his truck and looked at Carl. "Well, you know. It was kinda like he was nervous or scared or something. Like he wanted me to hurry up and leave. He was just real jittery. I could tell just by lookin' at him that he was up to somethin' he shouldn'ta been."

Marc looked Billy dead in the eyes. He knew the best way to tell if a person was telling the truth was to watch the eyes. Eyes always told it all, and many a deceptive person had been revealed by trained eye contact. "Was this man carrying anything? Did he have anything with him that you could see?"

"No, nothing other than his backpack. He threw that in the front of the Blazer."

Marc and Carl looked at each other, but neither spoke. The evidence against Foster was mounting quickly.

Marc turned back to Billy. "What made you want to talk to this man when you saw him here?"

Billy grinned. "I thought I recognized him and if he'd talk much, I'd ask him where all the deer are feedin'."

Marc looked puzzled. "I'm afraid you've lost me."

"I thought I'd seen him before. That's why I wanted to talk to him to see where the deer are grazin'. I was right too. It was him all right. I'd seen him before when I was up in the mountains scouting for deer. Never actually talked to him 'cause mountain people can be right funny about things like that. But I know it was him."

Marc was even more puzzled. "You've told this to the police and they still haven't moved on it?"

Billy grinned. "Yeah. Like I said, the chief don't believe me. He thinks I'm just a scatterbrained teenager. Well, I ain't."

Marc wasn't about to let the conversation drop. "I can see that. Could you tell me exactly where you saw Puckett?"

"Sure, it's up in the National Forest high up in the Ozarks. That's where it was."

Carl intervened. "Did Puckett have a camp set up or something?"

Billy laughed. "Camp hell, he has a cabin that looked like he built it hisself."

Marc grew impatient. "Billy, are you sure?"

"I'm tellin' you true, mister. I seen the guy. I'd

know him anywhere. He didn't know me 'cause he didn't see me when I seen him."

Marc took a deep breath. "Can you give us some directions to this place, Billy?"

"That's your truck over there, right?"

Marc answered. "Yes, why?"

"Sure is pretty and I'd love to take a ride in it. I'll tell you now, though, you ain't gonna get to that place in the mountains with that truck. Only way you can get to Puckett's cabin is walk or take one of them fancy ATV four by fours."

"If we promise you a ride in the rig, will you give us directions to Puckett's camp?"

"Hell, Mr. Lee, if you don't mind a good walk in the mountains, I'll make you a deal. You give me a ride in that big truck and I'll take you right to the rascal's door stoop."

Chapter Fourteen

David Foster found it difficult to sleep in the daylight. He attributed his uneasiness, in part, to having captured the man who had killed his family. Since he had been in the mountains, he had hardly ever slept beyond the first light of morning. Perhaps it had something to do with the intensity of the darkness at night in an area so far away from the influences of man's nighttime illumination devices, or perhaps it was the conflict raging within him that demanded resolution.

Foster sat up on his bunk and rubbed his eyes. He glanced at his wristwatch—quarter past ten. His arms went up over his head and he stretched to stimulate his lazy circulation. The strenuousness of the last twenty-four hours had certainly taken its toll. Foster felt tired, but the more he thought about Larry Cummings the more determined he was to exact his just reward from the murderous truck-driving druggie. In the meantime, much remained to be done.

Foster got up from the bed and stretched one more time. He took several deep breaths and looked around the one-room cabin for his boots. They were by the door where he had left them, so he quickly grabbed them and slipped them on. He ran his fingers through his shaggy hair and moved to the small kitchen area on the left side of the cabin.

Time for coffee.

Foster pumped the tank on the two-burner Coleman camp stove with the integral pump and twisted the burner knob on. He struck a kitchen match and lit the burner. Once it was burning to his satisfaction, he grabbed his coffeepot, filled it with spring water from the PVC makeshift tap, and set the pot on the burner. He found the percolator cup, put in his usual three teaspoons of coffee, placed the percolator cup inside the coffeepot, and closed the lid. In ten minutes, it would be ready and that was enough time to make a fast check on Cummings.

Foster grabbed the Ruger .22 automatic and stuffed it into his waistband. In seconds he was outside and moving toward the cage that housed Cummings. It wasn't surprising to see Cummings in exactly the same position he had left him. The overdose of diazepam had proven exceptionally effective, and Foster felt a sense of pride in conquering his hated prey so easily. His face split in a broad smile because the best was yet to come. Soon, Cummings would regain consciousness and the real fun would get underway. And for the grand finale, Larry Cummings would have a conscious sample of hell a few minutes before he actually got there. The same hell he had inflicted on Foster's innocent family. His only regret was that Larry Cummings had but one life with which to pay his morbid debt. But what Cummings could not give through his life, he would certainly repay with his pain. David Foster committed himself to that.

Foster rested his hands on the cage and looked hard at Cummings's motionless body on the floor of the cage. "Wake up, you bastard. It's payday."

The mountain was alive now with the sounds of birds chattering, squirrels cutting hickory nuts, and insects busy seeking their sustenance. David Foster made ready also. He walked to a large pile of cut oak, ash, and hickory saplings. He studied the pile and then the small clearing fifty yards from the cabin. There he would build the final monument to his torment and rid himself of the evil one who had taken everything of importance from his life. He had waited for over two years, so he decided he could wait until after he ate a hardy breakfast before starting the construction. Hard work always came easier on a full stomach.

By the time Foster returned to the cabin, the coffee was ready. He removed the pot from the Coleman stove and put a small pot of water on the burner. While he waited for the water to heat, Foster poured himself a cup of hot coffee and placed it on the wooden table he had built from abandoned wooden sawmill slats. He took a package of freeze-dried eggs and bacon from one of his nylon packs and put the package on the table beside coffee. Foster had come to appreciate the convenience, the nutrition, and the taste of freeze-dried meals. He always made it a point to keep plenty of variety in stock for a tasty and fast meal. He considered the nutritious meals to be a luxurious supplement to his diet normally harvested from the abundance of edibles found in the forest.

The water on the Coleman burner bubbled quickly. Foster ripped the top from the package and poured a sufficient amount of water into the aluminum-lined container. Then he stirred it and put it against a wooden candle holder on the table. In less than two minutes he would enjoy eggs and bacon, and he had decided to top the morning meal off with a slab of cured wild boar harvested earlier in the year from a ridge higher up in the mountains.

Foster sipped his coffee and then poured the contents from the freeze-dried food package into a camp cook kit plate on the table. He savoured his first bite when the sound startled him.

A scream. And it came from somewhere near the cabin.

Cummings?

Foster jumped from the table, instinctively going low in a crouch and doing a duck-walk across the floor until he reached one of ten gun ports he had built into the cabin walls. He chose the one nearest the cage where, only minutes earlier, he had left Larry Cummings sleeping. He scanned the perimeter for the source of the sound, hoping it would come again.

It came.

Cummings.

Foster eased up into position, the Ruger in his right hand and the safety off. Definitely Cummings. He was not only conscious, he was in a wild, screaming rage, shaking the wooden bars that were his prison.

Cummings was loud enough to alert anyone within a mile. "Where am I? What is this place? Somebody answer me."

David Foster wasn't worried, the nearest living human being was at least twenty miles away. Cummings could scream all he wanted to.

Foster returned to the table and shook his head. He picked his fork up and ate the reconstituted scrambled eggs and bacon. "Must have miscalculated the dosage," he said softly aloud as he sipped coffee to wash the delightful eggs down. "The asshole shouldn't have come to for a couple more hours. Ah, such cooperation. I'll simply start his due process earlier. Much earlier. It's time Larry Cummings got what's coming to him . . . everything that's due."

———

Marc Lee silently hoped Billy Kershaw's credibility wasn't deserving of Chief Miller's scorn. But for the last forty-five minutes, he would have sworn they were lost somewhere in the Ozark Mountains. And that presented a touchy situation because it wasn't simple to turn an eighteen-wheeler around on just *any* road. Thus far he had seen only one place that looked suitable for a turn-around, and that place was now at least three miles behind them. "Are you sure this is the road you wanted to take?"

Billy Kershaw was very confident. "Yeah, this is the place. There's a place you can stop this thing about a mile further out the road. We're gonna have to hoof it after that. Ain't no way on this green earth you're gonna get this truck up in them woods. It's too damn pretty a truck and besides that, it won't fit. The road gets real steep and narrow up ahead."

Carl looked at Kershaw and grinned. "You point to the right trail or even in the right direction and we'll furnish the transportation."

Kershaw shot back. "The good Lord done furnished our transportation. I done told you once, they ain't no way you're gonna git into them hills 'cept on foot. Less, of course, you got one of them ATV four-by-fours tucked away in one of your pockets."

Carl's grin broke into a full smile for a second, and then his face went cold again.

Marc looked at Kershaw. "How long ago were you in this range of the mountains, Billy?"

"Ain't been long. I always do me some early scoutin'. There's some mighty big old bucks that live up in the high country if you're a mind to walk in there after 'em."

Marc laughed. "Walkin' in was never the problem for me. Walkin' out with the buck always seemed to be the one that got me."

Billy stared out the windshield. "That clearin's just around the next bend. Get ready to stop. We're gonna have to burn some shoe leather from here on out."

Marc let it ride, forcing a silent smile and then returning his attention to the narrow gravel road. The Leeco rig moved slowly as Marc threaded it along the road. He reached the bend Kershaw indicated, and the rig twisted around it. In front of them now, lay a large, flat clearing. Marc maneuvered the rig into the clearing and stopped. He looked at Kershaw, who was sitting beside Carl on the edge of the passenger's seat. "How much further from here?"

"A mile, maybe a mile and a half. It's right mean country once we leave the road. What are you boys gonna do with Puckett if he's up there?"

Carl answered. "Try to bring him back. The man has hurt innocent people. He has to be held accountable."

Kershaw turned and studied the big warrior's face. "You guys cops or something?"

"No," Marc said.

"Oh," Kershaw replied, and he let it ride.

"Pathfinder, this is Barnburner. Are you there?" Brittin Crain's voice blared from the Icom speaker before anyone got out of the cab.

Marc reached for the microphone and answered. "Go. This is Pathfinder."

"Got some preliminaries for you. Pathologist's report just came in on Glen Hawthorn. He died from a single gunshot wound to the face. A twenty-two. He had a trace of drugs in his system, only they were prescription medications prescribed by his physician. It's a match with the prescription found in his travel bag. A combination of pseudoephedrine hydrochloride and acetaminophen. The man was taking sinus medication. Other than that, nothing. Did you copy?"

Marc hesitated and his face filled with a mixture of sadness and anger. He keyed the transmitter. "Affirmative. You got anything else?"

"One more thing. We also have preliminaries from the postmortem on the driver found at the rest area near Fort Smith. He died from chemical toxins. Best the computer can tell at this point, it was a mixture of poisonous substances derived from Angel of Death and Fly Amanita mushrooms. Clever and lethal. Foster is no dummy, he knows what he's doing or he's made some damned lucky guesses. Also, that driver tested positive for three different controlled substances including marijuana and amphetamines. He was a druggie. You got anything?"

Marc transmitted. "Affirmative. We have an eyewitness who saw Foster. He has taken us into the Ozark National Forest. He knows where the guy is or at least he thinks he does. If we find anything to indicate he's in these mountains, we're goin' in after him. If we're lucky, maybe Cummings is still alive. Then again, if Cummings is lucky, maybe he isn't."

There was silence for a long moment, and then Brittin Crain responded. "Can you give me an exact location?"

Marc replied quickly. "Look to the bird and we'll activate the chirp." Marc reached to his left wrist and activated the ultrahigh frequency digital transponder built into his wristwatch. The transponder immediately transmitted an encoded signal similar to aircraft beacons used to locate downed aircraft. The signal would be received by ComSat-D in orbit high above the earth. In seconds Delta Force command would be able to pinpoint his location within ten feet virtually anywhere on earth, and then the information could be relayed to Brittin Crain.

"Affirmative. We'll get a fix on your location and start some air support that way."

"Roger. Keep the air units away from the immediate location unless we call for them. We don't want to spook Foster if he's in these mountains. I'd like to bring him out alive."

"Affirmative," Crain replied. "You say the words and I'll send in the birds."

Marc smiled and pressed the push-to-talk switch. "You never lose that mild sense of humor, do you?"

The speaker crackled. "I try. If I get anything else, I'll ring your chimes. Barnburner clear."

"Affirmative. Pathfinder clear." Marc replaced the microphone and turned to Carl. "You feelin' lucky?"

Carl's face hardened. "Let's get it done. If our boy is in there, we gotta take him down before he kills again. If he hasn't already."

Marc and Carl climbed from the Leeco cab, followed by Billy Kershaw. They walked to the rear of the trailer, and Marc entered a digital sequence on a handheld transmitter. The doors opened and the hydraulic ramp decended.

"Holy shit!" Kershaw said when he saw the interior of the Leeco trailer complete with two Jeep Cherokees. "What is all this? What are you guys?"

"Truck drivers," Carl said. "Just truck drivers."

"Bullshit!" Kershaw replied. "I ain't never seen anything like this."

Marc went into the rear of the trailer by way of the ramps. "Let's off-load the Jeeps and we'll take the ATVs."

Kershaw stood wide-eyed while Marc and Carl removed the Jeep Cherokees from the rear of the trailer. In less than a minute, both machines were unloaded. Next, the Highway Warriors went to the storage facility outside the control room and released the safety-retaining straps that held both customized all-terrain vehicles. They fired the engines and drove the ATVs from the trailer.

Marc went back inside and entered the control room. He activated the communications equipment to link the Icom U-16 and H-16 handhelds to the Harris radio transmitter and the K-band uplink to ComSat-D. With the on-board repeater link in place, the Warriors could activate and link with Brittin Crain or Delta Force command by way of the small handhelds. The transceivers inside the rig would receive the signal from the handhelds and retransmit them at much higher power to the earth-orbiting defense department satellite.

When that was finished, both men ran thorough checks of the armaments and munitions for the ATVs. They selected weapons from the arms safe inside the rig, opting for M16s over the shorter range Uzis due to the terrain. Both men strapped on their utility belts and checked the Smith & Wesson 5906s for full magazines and chambered rounds.

Marc looked at Carl while he checked his weapons and extra ammunition. "Better activate your transponder just in case we get separated up there."

Carl pressed the switches on his wristwatch and activated his transponder to ComSat-D. He surveyed the terrain and looked at Kershaw. "Billy, are you sure this is the place?"

"Yeah. Positive. If he's up here, his Blazer will be parked in some cut brush 'bout a quarter mile up the road. Listen, ain't these four-bys gonna be loud up in the woods?"

Marc grinned and switched the exhaust system to whisper mode, and the running ATV fell almost totally silent. Carl did likewise, and the sound of the powerful off-road vehicles almost vanished.

"Damn!" Kershaw said, then shook his head in amazement.

Marc handed Kershaw a helmet and the teenager put it on. "Hop on behind me and hold tight. I'm counting on your lead. These mountains look really dense. Are you sure you remember the way?"

"Positive. I know these mountains as good as I know my own backyard. You drive and I'll get you there."

———

David Foster finished breakfast and cleaned his eating utensils under the flow of the diverted spring water in his makeshift kitchen. He checked the Ruger's position at his hip and walked outside.

Larry Cummings was gripping the wooden bars that contained him when he saw David Foster. He yelled as loudly as he could. "Who the hell are you? What do you want with me? I don't even know you."

Foster didn't answer, but he walked toward the cage. When he stood three feet from it, he stopped. Foster smiled a facetious smile. His voice was low and cold, haunting. "I trust you had a comfortable nap. I almost lost you once or twice. You should be most happy that I didn't. I know *I* am. Your loss would certainly be a blow to my ego. We have so much to discuss, you and me. If you find your accommodations a little less than desirable, well, tough shit. You'll get accustomed to it if you last that long."

Cummings's face went pale. He gripped the wooden bars even harder. "For God's sake, who are you?"

Foster looked at the caged man and grinned. Suddenly, his face became cold and filled with vengeance. "I am your tormentor. I am the delivery system for the punishment you deserve. I am the collector of the debt you owe. I am your present and your future. I am your educator and I will teach you a lesson unlike any you have ever learned. If you are fortunate enough and strong enough to live through it, then you will recognize me as the master of your destiny." Foster laughed uncontrollably now. "And when, my fine opponent, when it is finished, I shall then be your undertaker and the caretaker of hungry buzzards. That's who I am."

Cummings went into shock. He gasped for breath and his face was ashen-blue. "My God, you're crazy. You're nuts, aren't you? You're some crazy maniac. Man, you've had too many drugs. You're gone."

Foster stood silent for a moment. "Yeah, maybe I am. Maybe I'm all those things. But you know what, I'm gonna live to walk out of this mountain and I'm gonna take care of piles of shit like you. Society doesn't need you. You're a menace."

"Man, what is this? What have I ever done to you, huh? I never laid eyes on you until you bummed a ride. What's this about? You owe me that much."

Foster was angry and he slammed his fist against the cage. He shouted with the ferocity of a lion. "I owe you nothing! You owe me! I'll tell you what you owe me— your life, that's what. Does the name Foster mean anything to you?"

Cummings felt his legs go limp. He slumped down to the bottom of the cage. "Foster?" His voice mellowed and became soft. "What about the name Foster?"

David Foster stepped away from the cage. "Yeah, I

thought it would. I'll tell you about Foster. My name is David Foster. Ring any bells?"

Cummings nodded his head to indicate yes.

"I thought so. Two years, four months, five days, twenty-three hours, and nineteen minutes ago you met my family. You weren't as pleasant as I've been. You crashed into them in a drug-induced stupor and you killed them. But you couldn't just kill them and let them die; you made them burn and suffer. I've lived with that since ten minutes after the crash. And the courts saw fit to let you get back out among society, and you can even still drive a truck and take your drugs and you live your life like nothing ever happened. Well, you son of a bitch, it did happen and my family is dead. They're dead because self-gratification meant more to you than reasonable safety. You and your kind who take drugs and get out on the highway . . . it's got to stop. I'm going to stop you!"

Cummings was in tears and struggling for breath. "I'm sorry. I don't know what else to say. It was an accident—I swear it—an accident."

Foster had turned cold again. "That doesn't make my family any less dead. I guess the drugs were an accident too, huh?"

"No, I took 'em. I shouldn't have, but I did. I still do. I can't get it out of my system. I've tried. I swear I've tried. The stuff won't turn me loose. You don't understand what it's like. You couldn't. It's like a beast with its jaws clamped around your body and it won't let go of you. The more you struggle with it, the more it hurts. I'm sorry about your family. I didn't mean to hurt them, honest. They were just in the wrong place at the wrong time, that's all."

Foster's face was fiery red. He stared at Cummings, and then he broke into hysterical laughter. "So were you."

"What?"

"When I found you at that truckstop and I heard

your name. I knew someday we'd meet face to face, but I wasn't quite ready. It happened early. When I found you, you were just at the wrong place at the wrong time. Your luck ran out."

"What are you going to do with me?"

"Make you suffer like you've made me suffer. Give you a taste of the fear and the horror you gave my wife and two children. Let you feel the fire like you made them feel. And when I'm finished with that, I'm going to hurt you."

Foster turned and walked back to the cabin. He returned with a metal fuel can and a roll of toilet tissue. He found a stick in front of the cabin and stuck the toilet tissue roll on the end of it. Then he opened the can and saturated the roll with kerosene. He reached into his pocket and came out with a Bic disposable lighter. He flipped the striker wheel and the lighter glowed. Foster passed the flame under the soaked roll of tissue until it caught fire. Black smoke poured from the burning fuel and trailed skyward. Foster smiled and walked back toward the cage.

Cummings's eyes were opened wide in fear and disbelief. He scrambled for cover inside the cage, but there was none.

Foster was there now, standing and holding the burning makeshift torch. A sardonic look filled his face. He eased the burning object through the bars toward Cummings's face. When Cummings shoved himself back as far as he could to escape the torture, Foster laughed. "It's time. Now don't flake out on me yet. There's still a lot more to come. Don't try to fight it either, because I am your master. Your destiny has come for you. This is a small sample of what hell is like. I hope you enjoy it as much as you enjoy your drugs."

Chapter Fifteen

Billy Kershaw pointed to a clump of dried, cut brush. "Yep, there's his Blazer just like I thought it'd be. I knew it."

Marc slowed the high-tech, heavily armed ATV. "Did you report this to anyone when you spotted Foster up in the mountains?"

Kershaw loosened his grip around Marc's waist. "Naw. I figured to each his own, if you know what I mean. People come in here all the time and make a temporary place to stay. Ain't nothin' new, 'cept it's against the law. Them forest rangers get real torn outta whack if they catch somebody up in here cuttin' trees and stuff. Any camp, aside from a loggin' camp or somethin', is supposed to be temporary, and you gotta have a permit for it. I didn't think nothin' of it, really. Besides, I don't know if Puckett, uh, you call him Foster, I didn't know if he's the one that built the cabin or if he just sort of took it over from somebody else while they wasn't here."

Marc surveyed the Blazer. Foster had made good his attempt to hide it from both the ground and the air. The cut limbs and branches camouflaged it quite well. Marc shut the engine off on the ATV and dismounted. "You wait here, Billy, until I've checked-out this vehicle. Don't leave the seat. Is that understood?"

"Yes, sir, Mr. Lee."

Marc swung the M16 around on its sling and grabbed the pistol grip. The M16's stock rested on his hip as he moved toward the Blazer. His right index finger cradled the trigger.

Carl let his off-road machine idle and pointed the front of the ATV toward the covered vehicle so the .223 miniguns would be on-line if necessary. The position would also give the advanced electronics on the ATV an opportunity to scan the Chevy. Carl pressed the activation switch for the advanced infrared heat sensors. "Nothin' showing on the infrared scan, Marc. It's been here awhile. The scan says nobody's in it."

Marc moved cautiously toward the Blazer despite the fact that Carl's scanner indicated it was clear. He dropped low in a crouch and slipped alongside the 4 X 4 truck. The M16 was ready as Marc slowly moved his head up high enough to see inside the vehicle.

Nothing there . . . nothing except a blue tarp in disarray on the floor in front of the backseat. And that's exactly what Billy Kershaw had said Foster used to cover the man he placed in the backseat at the shopping center.

Marc turned back toward Carl and Billy Kershaw. "Bingo! We got our blue tarp. This is our boy."

Carl shut the engine off on his ATV and jogged to the Chevy, his M16 dangling from the black nylon web strap across his shoulders. "Okay, if this is our mark, what's the plan?"

Marc rubbed his chin for a minute and then snapped his fingers. "Remember in Grenada out near the airport when we had the sniper on the hill?"

"Yeah, good one. What did we call that, the reverse switch and takedown?"

Marc nodded his head. "Damn good plan as I recall."

"It worked without a hitch down there. Don't see why it won't here."

Marc yelled for Billy Kershaw. "Billy, come over here for a minute."

Kershaw left the ATV and joined Marc and Carl,

who were squatting over an area the size of a marble ring in the dirt.

Marc took a stick and drew an imaginary perimeter on the ground. "I've got to ask you some more questions about the layout of Foster's encampment. Do you remember it well enough to tell us a few things?"

"Sure, ain't much to it 'cept a cabin and some pole sheds he's got around it. Not too much to remember."

"Tell us how it's laid out. Which direction it faces and that sort of thing. Can you do that?"

"Sure thing." Kershaw found his own dried twig and sketched Foster's camp on the ground. When he was finished, he spent five minutes explaining the layout of the land around the cabin and the designation of each structure.

Marc and Carl studied the layout and listened attentively.

Marc looked up from the drawing. "How close did you get to the cabin when you saw Foster?"

"Oh, seventy-five to eighty yards. But I know it was the same man 'cause I looked at him through my binoculars. I watched him for half an hour. He was working on one of the sheds when I seen him. He's a hard worker."

"How big are these buildings?" Carl asked.

Kershaw could feel the excitement building, and his mind was bubbling. He hadn't known this much excitement since his first date with Jennie Moore. "Not very big. They're little storage sheds without a front on 'em. More like a lean-to than a real building."

"Is there more than one way out of here from the cabin?" Carl asked.

"Not without crossing over the upper ridges and fording the river on the other side. Puckett built his cabin about a hundred yards due east of an old logging trail. Not much of it left now. It's mostly grown up with scrub brush. You can still find it if you know where to look. That trail runs to the top of the mountain, and it starts about a hundred yards up that way." Kershaw pointed northeast of the location where the Blazer was parked. "That's about the only way out unless you got wings."

Marc looked at Billy and withdrew his stick from the ground plot. "Billy, it's against my better judgment, but we're going to take you in with us. You know these mountains, and anything might happen. David Foster is a desperate man. He's killed innocent people and it doesn't bother him. When we get close to his cabin, we'll drop you off. I want you to find a secure place and lay low. Don't leave until you see one of us come for you. You're a very helpful young man and I wouldn't want anything to happen to you. Do you understand me?"

Kershaw's face split wide with a smile. "Yes, sir, Mr. Lee. You can count on me doing whatever you tell me."

"It could get real nasty up there, Billy," Carl said. "Marc's right, you've got to do exactly what we say. It's for your own safety. There could be some shooting, although we'd like to take him down before it comes to that. We want David Foster alive and we want to get Larry Cummings out of there alive if he still is. We have your word?"

"You got it. You guys are really cops, aren't you?"

"No," Carl said. "We're men who have seen enough bloodshed at the expense of innocent and decent people. We want to do our part to stop it."

Kershaw looked puzzled. "You're vigilantes then?"

"Oh, no," Marc said. "We're patriotic citizens who happen to have some knowledge about how to get things done. We drive a truck for a living just like four million other men and women. Let it ride at that, okay?"

Billy pursed his lips and nodded his head. "Okay," he said, but he didn't buy it for one second. Even a fool could see these men were too well equipped and too proficient to be laymen. No doubt about it, they were professionals.

Marc stood from the imaginary perimeter on the

ground. "Okay, one last check of weapons and systems and then let's go get it done."

———

Larry Cummings cowered down in one corner of his cage and whimpered like a scolded puppy. His legs and arms burned, and twice he had slapped the fire out that devoured parts of his clothing.

David Foster watched the cowardly exhibition and laughed. "Doesn't feel so good, huh, Cummings? No, it doesn't. Think how my son and my daughter felt when they saw fire coming at them. Think what terror they felt before they were devoured like the thread in your pants. You think about that, Larry Cummings. When you rub your burns today and tomorrow and the next day, you think how two young children felt when their innocent flesh burned off their bodies. Yeah! If you want something for pain, I can give you that. I've got some drugs, Cummings. Remember how much you like drugs? How about it? You want drugs? Sure you do, something nice to help you stay awake like you do when you're driving on the highway. Want something?"

Cummings grabbed his legs and tried to make the burning go away, but it wouldn't. He looked at David Foster through teary eyes, but he didn't answer.

Foster became irate. He screamed. "I'm talking to you, Cummings! When I talk to you, you listen. When I ask you a question, you answer me. Do you hear me?"

Cummings nodded his head.

"Good. Remember, I am the master of your destiny. We can enjoy this together or I can become the personification of your worst nightmare. It's your decision."

Cummings found both the strength and courage to speak. "What do you want from me?"

"I told you before, your life."

"Kill me then. Go ahead, kill me and get it over. Be done with it. Kill me!"

"No, no, no. Not yet. We have so much to enjoy

before I let you go into the silent darkness. I want you to experience death before you actually die. I want you to know something like the horror my family felt in the instant between the time your rig slammed into their van and the time death finally took them away. I want you to have time to feel that . . . to understand it."

Cummings struggled for words, and the pain kept stinging him, punishing him. "What happened was a mistake. I admit that. I'm sorry. You have to listen to me. Nothing you or I can do will make them come back to you again. Nothing."

Foster walked around the cage in circles. He lifted a small section of vine from the ground. A handle made from a stick of wood was tied to each end. An improvised garrote. He held it steadily while Larry Cummings watched his movement. Suddenly, Foster plunged his hands through the wooden bars and wrapped the garrote around Cummings's neck. He jerked and twisted at the same time. The force of his motion lifted Cummings off of the ground.

Cummings fought for air, and his hands reached futilely for the vine that choked him. He gasped, and he could feel the veins protruding in his temples as his air supply shut down.

Foster pulled harder. Cummings was against the bars now and Foster tightened the grip. "Ah, now you have a sample of how it feels to smother. Unpleasant, isn't it. A little something else to think about . . . how my family felt when the fire and the smoke took the air away from them. Do you wonder, or do you know now? I've wondered. Yes, sometimes I've wondered all night long. Sometimes I've laid awake and felt tears in my eyes and I've wondered what they felt like. Does it hurt? Are you suffering? I certainly hope you are."

Cummings didn't answer because he couldn't. His face was turning bluish-black. His hands struggled to get a grip on the vine that choked him. Then the struggle ended and Cummings's hand fell limp to his sides an instant before his body collapsed to the ground.

Foster let go of the vine on one end and pulled it and his arms back from the cage. "You're such a sport, Larry. Pleasant dreams."

The garrote had stayed on long enough to render Cummings unconscious, but, aside from a sore neck, he would sustain no lasting injury from the encounter. When he woke up, Foster had a new surprise in store for him.

There hadn't been time, at the crack of dawn, to properly store the ATV when David Foster had arrived at the cabin. He took the opportunity now to move the machine behind the cabin to the entrance of a cave by the creek. He had tried to plan ahead for any contingency. The tunnels in the cave connected to a trapdoor in the cabin that he had constructed for an event that might necessitate a swift and silent departure from the camp. The distance between the cabin and the cave entrance at the creek was just short of fifty yards. The entrance was naturally camouflaged by a deadfall oak tree that securely shielded it. Foster had discovered the cave by accident during his first month in the mountains when a wounded squirrel had sought cover in the dried deadfall foliage.

Foster straddled the ATV and fired the engine. He drove down the ridge behind the cabin and stopped at the cave's entrance. Once the dried foliage was moved, he backed the ATV into the secure opening and replaced the dried limbs and leaves.

It took five minutes to hike back up the steep incline to the cabin. When he got there, Larry Cummings was still unconscious, but gasping for breath. Foster unlocked the padlock and grabbed Cummings by the upper arms. He moved him haphazardly toward the cabin. Foster backed inside when he reached the door, tugging Cummings's arms until the man crossed the threshhold. Once inside, Foster lowered Cummings to the floor and opened the trapdoor. Beneath the door, an eight-foot wooden ladder led to the bottom of the cave's tunnel. Foster picked Cummings up in a fireman's carry, climbed through the door, and down the ladder.

Five feet away from the cabin entrance, the cave was totally black. Foster twisted the head of his mini-MagLite and the cave came to life. He moved forward in the narrow channel until he reached a larger opening almost as large as the cabin. He laid Cummings down on the damp floor and lit a kerosene lantern he had stored there earlier. Foster immediately took a four-foot piece of rope from his pocket and securely tied Larry Cummings's hands behind his back, slipping the rope through Cummings's belt loop so he couldn't manipulate his arms to the front of himself. He used a second piece of rope to tie his legs at the ankles and the knees. When Foster was satisfied the ropes would hold, he picked up a paintbrush from an open can and dipped it in a thick, gellike mixture of pine resin and turpentine. He slopped the mixture on Cummings's clothing one brushful at a time until the gel covered him. When the turpentine evaporated, the pine resin would still adhere to Cummings. The coating of one of nature's best natural incendiaries would potentially make Cummings a living torch. With the flick of a burning stick match, Larry Cummings could be reduced to toast . . . contingency plan B. Foster blew the kerosene lantern out and headed back to the cabin.

In little over a minute, he was back inside the comfortable one-room living quarters. He poured himself a second cup of coffee, sipped it, and walked outside. He took a deep, cleansing breath of fresh mountain air and stretched his arms. His woodsman ax stood against the front of the cabin at the end of the porch. Foster looked at it and smiled. When Larry Cummings came to, it would be time to surgically remove a couple fingers. A mixture of roofing tar, brought to the camp from town, and pine resin would see that he didn't bleed to death, and the longer he could keep the druggie trucker alive, the more horror he could subject him to before he finally killed him.

Foster's empty hand wrapped around the ax handle and he lifted it over his shoulder. He turned for the cabin door and that's when he saw the reflection a hundred yards out into the forest. He got inside the cabin and quickly closed the door. He grabbed his Ruger Mini-14 and opened the gun port that faced in the direction of the reflection. He looked, but he didn't really see anything. As a precaution he energized the perimeter booby traps by connecting the wiring terminals to the spare twelve-volt battery he had for the ATV.

Foster looked hard, but he saw nothing that shouldn't be there. He waited, and while he waited, he scanned the forest with his binoculars. He saw it again, closer this time. It looked like a kid, and the reflection came from a gold medallion hanging on a neck chain that glittered in the sunlight.

Foster crammed the barrel of the Mini-14 through the gun port and touched off four fast rounds in the direction of the reflection. The kid disappeared, but immediately bits of the cabin's roof and ceiling fell to the floor from the impact of machine-gun fire. Foster hit the floor.

The forest was alive with a new sound. A public address system and the voice speaking into it sounded cold and hard. "David Foster, you are surrounded. Release Larry Cummings and step out of the cabin without your weapons. We don't want to harm you. If you continue to show force, we will be compelled to retaliate with greater force. We don't want to do that. Surrender now!"

———

Billy Kershaw ate dirt when the shots rang out. The projectiles slammed into the limbs above his head and then disappeared harmlessly through the forest.

Marc didn't take the opening barrage as a welcome sign. He returned fire with a long burst from the .223 Stinger miniguns on the front of his ATV. The sizzling death pellets chewed into the roof of the cabin. He had chosen the target intentionally to ensure Larry Cummings's safety if he was inside with Foster. The assault and rescue had already gone awry. But then Marc knew such things happened when textbook-theory encountered real-world activity. He had long ago decided that textbooks belonged in the classroom and not in the killing field. And despite Billy Kershaw's help, assurances, and good intentions, the young man lacked both the experience and the professionalism for this kind of assault. That's why the insurgence had gotten off-track—Kershaw didn't get down and stay down like he was told.

The lethal tiger had been unleashed and Marc knew there was only one way to play—Foster's way. He hoped Foster wasn't smart enough or he was too scared to realize it. The announcement on the ATV's PA had been a bluff—one Marc hoped might work. Deep in his gut, he knew it wouldn't.

Inside the cabin, David Foster eased himself up from the floor to the gun port. He scanned the forest for a sign of the intruders. There was none. Whoever they were, they had vanished after the first shots were fired. Foster knew they were still out there somewhere, and rather than wait for a massive insurgence he decided to make an attempt at escape.

Foster grabbed two spare magazines for the Mini-14. He also picked up his one souvenir of former active military service—a live hand grenade. He stared at the grenade for a long moment, and that's when he realized he had his ticket out.

Foster crawled on his stomach to the trapdoor and lifted it. He descended the ladder and reached the cave's dirt floor below. With the aid of his mini-MagLite, he reached Larry Cummings. The trucker was semiconscious and moaning. Foster knelt beside him after he lit the kerosene lantern. He removed a long piece of braided nylon cord from his pocket and threaded one end through the second buttonhole on Cummings's shirt. He pulled the shirttail out and moved the cord around Cummings's chest, bringing the end back through the buttonhole. Then he took both ends of the cord and tied them securely to the neck of the hand grenade beneath the lever. He pulled the ends tightly until the grenade rested firmly against Larry Cummings's chest, and then he tied them off. He took another piece of the nylon cord—about eight feet long—and threaded it several times through the safety pin on the grenade. Two half-hitches secured the cord to the pin. Foster looped the other end around his waist and tied it securely.

Cummings was regaining consciousness. He saw Foster in the dim glow of the lantern and jerked his head back.

"No, no," Foster said, and he shined the mini-Mag on Cummings's chest. "You'd better take a look at that first."

Cummings froze. His heart raced in fear and panic. His vision blurred, but his eyes opened wide and he gasped. "Oh, shit!"

"Not to worry," Foster said. "You be a good boy and we're both okay. Try to be a hero and we're both dead. You got that?"

Cummings nodded.

Foster grinned. "We have company outside. They want me to release you. Remember one thing—if I go down, you go with me. Understood?"

Cummings nodded again.

"Very good. Now, let's go." Foster cut the ropes binding Cummings's legs.

Cummings was still dazed, and he had no idea where he was. "Go? Where are we going?"

"Even the best-laid plans demand flexibility. We're going for a ride."

Chapter Sixteen

Carl had moved out at the first sound of gunfire. He ran due east, down the steep ridge in back of the cabin. In the bottom of the ravine, he crossed the cold mountain creek and headed up the ridge on the other side. If Foster made an escape attempt out the back of the cabin, Carl would be ready.

Marc moved north of the encampment at a cut clearing fifty yards from the cabin. He sat patiently, the ATV humming and the infrared scanner seeking body heat inside the building. It found none. Marc keyed the voice operated transmitter switch and spoke into the microphone in his helmet. "Bro, the scanner isn't showing anything inside. You see anything back that way?"

"Negative. He couldn't have gotten out. I've been on the backside since five seconds after the first shots were fired. He's got to be in there. Any sign of Cummings?"

"Negative."

"You think maybe he's already dead?"

Marc scanned the encampment carefully while he spoke. "Could be, but I figure if Foster was going to take him out this quickly, he'd have iced him in the truck instead of wasting time up here. My gut says he wanted to play with him first. Whoops, the metal detector is picking up charges all around the perimeter. Watch yourself."

"Affirmative."

"I'm gonna make some noise up here and see if we get a reply. Stand-by." Marc switched off the VOX transmitter and keyed the PA system. "Foster. This is your last chance. We're coming in after you."

Nothing.

Marc steadied the gunsight and unleashed a mini-rocket from the port tube. A blazing swoosh was followed almost immediately by a loud, earthshaking explosion. When the smoke blew away, the cage and one of Foster's lean-to sheds had vanished.

Still no reply from inside the cabin.

Carl's frantic voice crackled through Marc's headset. "I've got visual on him! He was in a cave. He's on an ATV. He's rolling . . . up the creek bottom. Cummings is sitting in front of him. I'm on him. Close from the top.

Marc kicked the ATV's throttle and the mighty 4 X 4 machine lurched to life. He ran hard to the edge of the ridge until he crossed over the crest and started down. He could hear Foster's ATV coming up the creek bed. Marc took cover behind a dense growth of mountain laurel and waited. When Foster was seventy-five feet from him, he popped the clutch, and his high-tech ATV jumped into the creek bed.

Foster slammed on his brakes and let off the throttle. He looked at Marc and then he looked behind him and saw Carl closing. He looked to his right, up the steep mountain slope, then back at Marc. He gripped the throttle in his right hand and twisted it as hard as he could. The three-wheel ATV's engine lurched back to life. Dry leaves and dirt flew in the wake of spinning rear tires. Cummings slammed back into Foster's chest from the unexpected acceleration as Foster tried to stabilize the ATV. The front wheel left the ground and tore through the air. Foster leaned forward, pushing Cummings toward the handlebars. Both men fought for balance. For their lives.

Marc followed Foster's lead. He throttled the high-tech ATV. The machine responded instantly with over-sized rubber tires pawing for traction against the torque of the sound-surpressed engine. Water flew as Marc's ATV plowed into the rocky bottom of the creek, devoured it, and clawed into the soft, dry ground cover on the other side. Marc tracked Foster through his infrared helmet utilizing the ISI infrared scanning imager built into the off-road apparatus. He steered the machine and tracked Foster at the same time, searching for the opening to divert Foster's escape. The ISI held steady, tracking Foster and Cummings aboard Foster's ATV. Marc gripped the firing mechanism with his left hand and led Foster's escaping vehicle by three or four feet. He unleashed a burst of warning fire into the ground ahead of Foster with the . 223 Stinger-type miniguns on the front fender flares of the machine. A trail of debris rose from the ground and sailed into the air as if a giant mole were burrowing beneath the soil toward Foster's machine at lightning speed.

Foster cut right, let off the throttle for an instant, then cut the handlebars hard left. He opened the ATV's throttle all the way, and the machine fishtailed right, then left.

Cummings struggled to keep his balance on the narrow seat. He felt the line leading to the grenade, his lifeline, tighten as he bounced like a rag doll against the force of the sudden turns. He knew if he lost his balance and fell, there would be no second chance. The grenade would detonate before he could move.

Carl saw Foster's escape effort before he had stopped his ATV when he came up behind him. He turned the machine up the mountainside in a trail parallel to Foster. The custom machine moved in a lightning whisper as Carl steered between trees and negotiated the forty-degree embankment. But now Foster had the upper hand. He had not only increased the distance between him and his pursuers, he also knew the terrain. And that was something neither Carl nor Marc had going for them.

Marc throttled up hard and tried to gain on Foster.

He ran past trees, dead brush, and young saplings that dotted the mountainside. Had it not been for Cummings on the seat in front of Foster, Marc would have simply launched a rocket at Foster's ATV and ended it. There was still a chance Foster could be taken alive, and as long as that chance existed, Marc would try to end the conflict peacefully. But first he had to catch the fleeing ATV.

Foster zigzagged through the underbrush, dodging trees and deadfall with skillful precision. He knew if he could make it to the top of the ridge, he could lose the men who chased him. An old logging road just over the crest of the knoll lead into a maze of other logging roads that challenged even those who were familiar with them. The ATVs could easily negotiate the roads, but keeping too close would be difficult. If he could make it to the road, the game would change. And when it changed, he would kill the men who wanted him just an instant before he killed Larry Cummings. That would come, but right now Foster realized for the first time since the insatiable hunger for revenge had consumed him that he was scared out of his mind. He knew he had to get away.

Carl spoke into the voice-operated microphone in the ATV helmet. "Bro, I'm going for the top of the ridge. I'll keep a fifty-yard spread from Foster and try to take him from up there."

Marc steered, ducked brush, and spoke into his VOX microphone while his ATV ate the mountainside. "Watch him. He's got an assault rifle over his shoulder. Looks like a Mini-14. If he decides to stop ahead of us, he could take a few pot shots. I'll try to herd him toward you."

"Roger," Carl replied as he twisted the handle bars to miss a stump concealed by heavy leaves. The machine responded quickly, and he narrowly missed the obstacle that could have overturned his ATV. "I don't want to take him with Cummings on the bike. If we can keep him hemmed in, maybe we can lay enough strafing fire to get him off the bike. We get him off and separated from Cummings, we can take him down. What say?"

Marc spoke into the VOX microphone again. "Affirmative. Remember, it's his mountain and he knows this turf. We've got to make the odds turn for us some other way. Over." The words had hardly cleared his throat when the ATV struck a hidden rock and swerved hard to the left on the left two tires. Marc followed the roll and cut to the left to regain control, the ATV almost tipping to its side in the process. The machine crashed through a growth of dense small trees and finally righted itself. Marc breathed hard and felt the adrenaline rush through him. He let off the throttle and coasted to a stop. Then he cut the front wheels sharply right and resumed his chase.

Carl glanced to his left and saw Marc almost lose the ATV. "Close there, bro. See you on top."

"Roger," Marc said. "Hang on to your ass. I'm gonna make some noise and see if I can rattle Foster's cage." He twisted the throttle for all he could get under the adverse terrain conditions. The off-road machine tore through leaves and dirt while it pawed its way toward Foster. Marc looked ahead, then locked Foster on target with the infrared imager. He moved the trajectory calculator with his left thumb and led Foster's ATV by ten meters. When he locked the imager on-line, he triggered a minirocket. A whoosh led a trail of spiraling smoke as the volatile projectile streaked toward the mountainside in front of Foster's machine.

The world erupted in front of Foster and Cummings. A loud explosion produced a burst of white, then orange, flames that caused debris to rain across the forest floor. Foster cut to his right, toward Carl, to avoid the crater left by the volatile impact.

Cummings screamed at the sound of the impact, his scream hidden beneath the earthshaking sound of the explosion. He lost his balance and felt himself brutally sliding from the seat. Then he felt the cord draw taunt that was attached to Foster's waist and the hand grenade. His eyes opened wide and he gasped for breath when he glanced down and saw the pin slip slightly on the grenade's trigger mechanism. And in a microinstant, Larry Cummings knew what hell was like because the devil behind him was guiding the tour.

———

Billy Kershaw heard the explosion on the other side of the ravine from where he hugged the ground. Foster's shots had paralyzed him mentally and physically. For the first time in his life, he understood the expression one of the regulars at the doughnut shop used frequently: "He didn't know whether to shit or go blind". And that was exactly how he felt at the moment. He was scared to run and afraid to stay where he was.

Kershaw stayed prone and listened. He could hear the sound of the ATV fading toward the top of the mountain ridge behind the cabin. He wasn't sure which was louder, the ATV's engine or the beating of his heart inside his chest. But something made sense. If the ATV was fleeing on the other side of the ridge and there had been an explosion, then that had to mean Foster or Puckett or whatever his real name was, was making a run for freedom.

He took deep breaths and tried to calm himself. The thoughts pounded inside his head with an intensity that almost equalled his frantically beating heart. The one thing he knew for certain was that he was too young to die.

If Foster made it to the top of the ridge and he could get to the logging roads, he could weave his way through the mountains until he ran out of fuel or decided to work his way out. He couldn't go far beyond the ridge on the other side because of the river that flowed through a giant gorge at the bottom of the mountain. The ATV might be fast in the forest, but it couldn't float.

Kershaw had an idea. If he could make his way to

the cabin, he might be safer there. Foster wouldn't likely return as long as Lee and Browne were chasing him. And if Foster had left the cabin hurriedly, he might have left something behind that could be used for a weapon. Right now, Billy Kershaw decided he would feel a lot more comfortable with something he could use defensively if he should happen to encounter Foster again. Anything would help.

He listened while the sound of the off-road machines climbed the ridge several hundred yards away. When he had suppressed his fear for safety, he jumped from the leaves and ran as hard as he could for the cabin door.

When Kershaw's feet landed on the wooden front porch to Foster's cabin, he stopped. He dropped his arms down and rested them against his knees as he struggled for breath. It took a moment or two, but normal breathing finally returned. He nudged open the hand-hewn wooden door and went inside.

"Wow!" he said as he scanned the interior of Foster's retreat. "This guy really knows how to escape from the world."

Kershaw picked up a small metal box with switches and lights on it. He scanned the labels above each switch. "Booby traps," he said. "This crazy bastard has the mountain wired with booby traps. Incredible! I could have been killed."

Foster steered the ATV through the hailstorm of dirt and debris. Cummings crashed against Foster's arms and made steering difficult. Foster managed to get control of the ATV by shoving Cummings from side to side. He blinked hard and squinted against the sunlight to see the top of the ridge. His eyes stung from the hard rain of dirt and wood splinters. And to make matters worse, Cummings was still screaming as he fought for balance on the ATV's seat.

"Shut up!" Foster yelled into Cummings's ear.

"Kill me, Foster," Cummings screamed. "Go ahead and kill me and be done with it. Those idiots on those four-wheelers are gonna kill both of us. Just do it and be done."

Foster had lost what little patience he had left. "Dammit, I said shut up. If those guys were going to kill us, they would have already done it. Keep your damned mouth shut and do what I tell you to do. You hear me?"

Cummings didn't answer.

The ATV leaped over a small embankment and landed on the logging road at the very top of the steep ridge. Foster glanced back and saw one ATV closing on him fast. He jerked his attention back to the road in front of him. His hand twisted the throttle, and the ATV lurched forward. But there was movement to his right. He chanced a fast glance and saw another ATV closing from his side.

Foster yelled into Cummings's ear again. "Hang on to your ass, Cummings. We're goin' for a run. Remember, you fall off and the grenade goes bang."

Cummings was far too scared to answer, but he kept wiggling the rope that bound his hands. And as long as Foster didn't find him out, there just might be a chance.

———

Marc's ATV was airborne when it cleared the top of the ridge and landed in the middle of the logging road. He cut the steering hard to the left to regain control. The machine spun sideways, fishtailed, then righted itself when he cut back to the right with the steering bars.

Carl hit the road a few feet in front of Marc, his machine stable when it landed in a cloud of dirt.

Marc spoke into the radio. "We can take him if the terrain levels out some. He knows the turf, but he can't outrun one of these machines."

Carl answered immediately. "Remember what

T. K. Davidoff said when he told us about these things: Don't let 'em get away from you."

"I got the scanner locked on Foster and the CAS is active. I still want to try and take him down without hurting Cummings," Marc said.

"I know a way," Carl replied as both ATVs chewed the leaf-covered ground in front of them. He jerked the throttle and his ATV shot far ahead of Marc's. "I'm gonna give him a buzz. When I get around him, we'll cut his ass off and take him down."

"I'm with you," Marc said the instant the squelch tail cracked through his headset.

Trees and low-lying brush streaked by and slapped their helmets as Marc and Carl closed the gap to Foster and Cummings.

"Watch him. He's got a gun on a strap around his shoulder," Marc said.

"I'm gonna make it so uncomfortable he'll have a hell of a time gettin' to that gun and drivin' at the same time," Carl replied. He streaked toward Cummings, saplings and dead weeds crashing to the ground in the wake of the mighty custom ATV.

Foster looked back. He saw Carl closing on him. His right hand stayed on the throttle while he cradled the Mini-14's pistol grip with his left. He shoved the muzzle rearward, his left arm cross-body. A burst of gunfire roared throughout the tranquil mountain over the buzz of the ATV engine.

Carl saw the movement coming. He zigzagged the high-tech ATV, and Foster's death fire flew harmlessly into the forest. Carl locked the ATV's scanner imager electronic sight on Foster's fleeing machine. "I'm gonna dump a little hellfire his way, bro," Carl said into the helmet microphone. "I'll try to take his tires out."

"Go for it," Marc replied. He was also closing now. His ATV sped through the forest creating little more sound than a mild wind whistling through leafless trees.

Carl fingered the firing mechanism, but something

happened and he released his finger before the Stinger miniguns erupted.

Foster cut the ATV hard left off the road. It bounced down the side of the mountain toward the creek. Cummings and Foster flopped up and down on the black vinyl seat of their machine. The off-road beast jumped stumps, rocks, and deadfall as it plowed a course deep into the ravine.

"He's running back toward the cabin," Carl yelled into the helmet microphone.

"I'm on him," Marc replied. He cut hard left with the custom off-roader and tunneled through the brush. The ride was reminiscent of his days on the Lee family farm in Dallas when he tried to break a young colt, back in some other lifetime. The machine bucked, jumped, settled for an instant, and bucked some more as it crashed down the rugged mountainside. For a short time, it seemed to have a mind of its own.

Marc steered hard. He saw Foster crashing down the mountainside to his right. In seconds, they were at the bottom of the ridge, across the creek, and up the other side.

"Where's he going?" Marc asked into the helmet microphone.

"Beats me," Carl replied. "I'm on his tail. Where are we?"

"Best I can calculate, we're headed for the ridge north of the cabin," Marc said. "We've got to get him down before he gets to the main trail out of here."

"Roger. I'm gonna try the buzz again," Carl replied. He twisted the throttle harder to close the gap. The ATV crashed through the undergrowth like a runaway army tank on some unknown course.

Foster looked to his left and saw one ATV running parallel to him. He chanced a fast glance to the rear and saw the other one closing behind.

Larry Cummings looked at the pin in the hand grenade attached to his chest. He fought to stay on the seat, his heart beating faster from overwhelming fear. The grenade bounced with each bump encountered by the ATV, jigging the pin nearly out of its socket. And Cummings was reminded yet again that death was staring him in the face . . . now only a quarter of an inch away.

———

Billy Kershaw heard it first. Then he looked out the north window inside the cabin and saw Foster's ATV break through the first clearing high up the ridge from the cabin. He held the metal box in his hands nervously. Kershaw wasn't sure what would happen if he flipped the switch labeled Northern Perimeter. Maybe something would happen and maybe it wouldn't. One thing Kershaw did know, Foster was coming toward the cabin. It was too late to run and too risky to stay.

With trembling fingers, Kershaw flipped the switch.

At first, it looked like a volcanic eruption. The side of the mountain opened up and regurgitated fire, dirt, and rock. Foster let off the ATV's accelerator and slammed on the brakes to avoid the crater that had appeared in front of him. The ATV slid into a U-turn and stopped.

Marc and Carl stopped their high-tech machines thirty yards from Foster and Cummings. Marc stared at him head-on and Carl sat forty-five degrees away, his finger resting on the firing mechanism. Through the optical scanner, Carl saw that he didn't have a clear line of fire. Cummings was in the way, and if Foster didn't move, Carl could do nothing from where he sat.

Cummings was shaking, and Foster's eyes widened as he stared at Marc and Carl. His hand rested around the pistol grip of the Mini-14.

No one moved.

Marc spoke into the microphone for the PA, his finger resting on the rocket-firing mechanism. "It's over,

Foster. Let's quit and go get this thing cleared up. You've hurt enough innocent people."

Cummings remained in front of David Foster on the ATV, his hands still bound behind his back, the white nylon braided cord still taut from the grenade's safety pin to Foster's waist. Cummings was pale as David Foster shouted over his shoulder. "Don't talk to me about innocent. This man killed my family. He's going to pay."

Marc's voice was cold. "Let him go, David. You've made too many mistakes. You've killed a cop and at least one innocent truck driver. I don't know how many more. You've reached the end of the road."

Foster yelled again. "All I've killed is a dumb cop who didn't understand shit, and drug-using truck drivers. They deserved to die. Cummings is rigged with a grenade. You take me out and he goes too. Now stay out of my way and let us out of here."

Marc was unyielding, his voice hard. "I can't do that. You killed a driver near Texarkana. He was on sinus medication. He was innocent. That man worked for me."

Foster was screaming. "Cummings murdered my family. This man and his drugs took everything I cared about in the whole world. This bastard has to pay."

Marc's voice blared across the PA. "I know all about that, and I'm sorry. Your family wouldn't want it to end this way. Don't do it, David."

Foster's trembling voice echoed through the Ozark Mountains. "Don't do it, huh? Don't do it, my ass. Tell me something, big man. What would you do if it happened to your family?"

Marc couldn't answer, and he lifted his finger off the firing switch.

Larry Cummings was trembling with fear. His life flashed by in a fleeting panorama, and he realized his drug use had been a serious and very costly mistake.

David Foster seemed to relax. His face bore a look of satisfied peace. He jerked the cord attached to the grenade's safety pin, and Larry Cummings screamed one final scream before the fiery holocaust consumed them.

After Foster's ATV burned out, Marc and Carl found Billy Kershaw and searched Foster's cabin. They found his array of chemical compounds and a funeral wreath with a dozen dried roses missing from one side. Carl looked at it sadly. "Must have been from his family's funeral," he said.

"It's tragic," Marc said. "Look how many roses are missing. I wonder how many killings we don't know about."

"We may never know," Carl said.

Marc turned to Billy Kershaw. "We're heavily indebted to you for this one, Billy. I'm not sure we would have found him without you. I have to admit, though, that explosion scared the hell out of me. How did you know when to hit the switch?"

Kershaw smiled. "I didn't. I just guessed. I didn't have no idea what would happen. Anyway, I'm glad it's over. You guys are incredible. I've never seen nothing like this."

Carl laid the wreath down and looked at Marc, his face serious. "When Foster asked what you would do, why didn't you answer him?"

Marc hesitated and stared vacantly around the cabin, his mind racing back to the beginning of this war so long ago at Leeco Freight Lines in Dallas. "Same reason you didn't, Major. Foster was insane. Maybe his motive was justified, I don't know. That's between him and his maker. Either way, his reckless method wasn't justified. I related to his feelings for an instant and I couldn't answer him. I couldn't stop him." Marc took a deep breath and looked away. "If it had been you stopped in front of him up there, what would you have said?"

ACTION ON EIGHTEEN WHEELS!

Marc Lee and Carl Browne, ex-Delta Force warriors and now the men of Overload: they've taken on the Mob . . . kill-crazy terrorists . . . deadly drug cartels . . . a nationwide, bloodthirsty Satanic cult—all child's play compared to their next mission!

HUNTSVILLE HORROR

The men of Overload are picked by the President of the United States to transport a lethal nuclear device to a top-secret research facility in Huntsville, Alabama. With the help of the super Overload rig, a safe delivery seems assured . . . only a heavily funded terrorist organization wants the device for its own deadly purposes! Before it's all over, Marc Lee and Carl Browne will face their most perilous challenge yet—and the six-lane highways of Alabama will be awash in blood!

Here's an exciting preview of Book #9 in the explosive OVERLOAD series

HUNTSVILLE HORROR
by
Bob Ham

Look for OVERLOAD wherever Bantam Books are sold.

Chapter One

General A.J. Rogers, III, commander of America's Delta Force, stood from behind the mahogany desk at the Pentagon in Washington, D.C. His round, pudgy face was flushed its normal red. When he spoke, his cheeks bounced in rhythm with his words. "Colonel Lee. Major Browne. I probably don't need to remind both of you that this mission is veiled in utmost secrecy. The President is scared shitless that some disgruntled bureaucrat is going to blow the lid off of this thing before the project is in place. That's why you're here. The President and I want to be damned sure nothing happens to this newfangled microreactor before it finds its way into orbit. If something goes astray, we'd all better plan to stow away on the next mission into outer space and then take a space walk without a space suit."

Colonel Marc Lee, Delta Force warrior turned Highway Warrior, managed a sheepish grin. "So we're dealing with a fire so hot that if anybody gets burned, we all burn? Is that the gist of it?"

"In a polite way, yes," General Rogers said.

"What are they gonna do with this thing once it's in space, General?" Major Carl Browne asked.

Rogers walked to the edge of his desk and sat down on the lip. "It's a microminiature nuclear reactor for use on America's orbiting space station. That is, in the event the thing ever becomes a reality. Some environmental group has scooped word of its existence and they plan to do whatever they can to stop its use in space. The government and NASA are denying its very existence . . . disclaiming it as nonsense."

"Uh," Carl said. "All this fuss over something small enough to fit into a suitcase. Amazing."

"Don't let the size fool you, Major," Rogers said. "That little device is capable of supplying all of the electrical energy necessary to run an entire space station for ten years without refueling."

"What will they do with it in Huntsville, General?" Marc asked.

"Run it through the paces before the space shuttle takes it into orbit in a couple of weeks. The launch date and time is classified. We don't know exactly when it will launch. That's not the problem, men. This reactor can be modified to form the heart of a chain-reactive nuclear device. Simply translated, this little gem could form the core for a major nuclear weapon. World situation what it is, there are a bunch of terrorists crackpots out there who would stop at nothing to get their hands on it. Hell of it is, if they accomplished that the thing could be flown right out of the country in somebody's luggage and no one would be the wiser. That *cannot* and *will not* happen. Understood?"

"Perfectly," Marc replied. "One question, sir."

"Yes?"

"Isn't this a little out of our normal line of work?"

Rogers cheeks jiggled with light laughter. "No, not at all. Sometimes the best way to fight crime is to prevent it. That's why you men will be transporting this device. There isn't a more secure or safer eighteen-wheeler than the Leeco rig in these United States. There certainly is no one more qualified to handle the security for something like this than you and Carl. There is no better way. Period."

Carl walked to the heavy bright metal suitcase sitting on a table across the room. He looked at the microreactor device, pushed on the foam padding that held it, turned, and faced General Rogers. "This thing looks like a stainless steel garbage disposal. Look at the way it's shaped. You're serious, this thing can run all the electricity needed for a space station for *ten* years?"

Rogers nodded. "Right, that's what they tell me. Ten years. And that's even without the supplementary support of solar panels. Hard to believe, isn't it?"

"Damn sure is, General," Carl said.

"Who builds this thing, General?" Marc asked.

"It's the creation of a little known outfit called STAR . . . Space Technology Advanced Research. They have a massive research, development, and testing facility built into the side of the Blue Ridge Mountains on the rural fringes of Roanoke, Virginia. Windy Gap mountain, I think it's called. Hardly anyone outside of government or NASA circles know they exist. I visited the facility once. You're right in the middle of it and you don't even know it's there. I found it spooky, to be perfectly honest. All that high technology research right under the noses of the locals and hardly anyone knows what really goes on inside that mountain. Probably for the best too. Some quack goes off and . . . well, you know how the scenario goes."

"All too well," Marc said. "When do we leave?"

"Now."

"Sounds good," Carl said. "I have one question, General."

"Yes, Major?"

"Who knows we're transporting this device?"

Rogers smiled and his cheeks jiggled again. "Good question. The President, me, and both of you. The scientists at Huntsville know only that someone will be making the delivery. They don't even know who or exactly when."

"So there shouldn't be any obstacles along the way?" Marc asked.

"You know the drill, Marc," Rogers said. "Never take anything for granted when you're dealing with this level of security. Anything is possible. Even the very best security clearances are not infallible. You both know that. But to answer your question, I don't anticipate any problems."

"Right," Marc said. The tone of his voice clearly indicated he wasn't convinced.

"One more thing," Rogers said. He walked to the metal suitcase and stared at the stainless steel nuclear device meticulously packaged in the foam supports. "I want one of you with this device at all times. Don't let it out of your control until it is turned over to the people at NASA down at the Cape when the tests are finished in Huntsville. Eat with it, sleep with it, and I don't give a damn if you try to make love to it . . . just don't let this thing get away from you. Whatever the costs."

"Yes, sir," Carl said. "You say this deal should be finished and the shuttle ready to launch in the next ten days. Is that right?"

"Ten days. Two weeks. Somewhere around there," Rogers said.

Marc looked at Carl and saw worry in the big black warrior's face. He sought to furnish reassurance. "We can handle it. Right, Carl?"

"Right, Colonel," Carl said reluctantly, his face tense and tight.

"Good, we have a few things to take care of and then let's go to Huntsville." Marc closed the lid on the suitcase and snapped the heavy duty latches shut. He secured the Medeco padlocks and then the Sargent and Greenleaf combination locks on the front of the hinges. "Alright, nice and secure. Combination memorized." He punched the digits on a digital keypad mounted on the outside of the case near the carrying handles, and a beep sounded. "Self-destruct detonator activated. Anybody messes with this little gem now without the proper key sequences and the combinations, and we'll all glow in the dark."

Carl's face hardened and every muscle in his body

drew tight. "Wonderful. That sure makes me feel better."

———

J. Dermont Ashland enjoyed being in control. It didn't matter whether it was his children's future or the future of his selfmade empire. Along with his abundant wealth came the special treatment he enjoyed so much. The aurora of superiority over everything he encountered, everything he touched. But even above his ability to control, Ashland enjoyed the veil of secrecy that clouded his financial megabase . . . Louisville, Kentucky.

Some of Dermont's closest and most trusted associates, although they were indeed quite few in number, felt that the old tycoon carried the mystique too far. So far, in fact, that few, if anyone at all, even knew that the J in his name stood for Jefferson. Dermont had dropped the "Jefferson" business during his childhood and insisted, when pressured, that his parents had merely used the initial J without further significance.

Ashland had come by his money the old fashioned way . . . hard work and shrewd business practices. The shining stars in his financial portfolio were Ashland Chemical and ATS . . . Ashland Transport Service. The name of the latter reaked of simplicity, but first glances were very far from the truth. ATS wove a complicated web of corporations and holding companies that controlled at least a score of medium-sized trucking concerns around the country. In the battle for financial dominance in Ashland's portfolio, ATS consistently perpetuated the old man's wealth by constantly returning a healthy bottom line. He had come from the coal mines of eastern Kentucky to the top floor of his own highrise in downtown Louisville. ATS had made the trip much easier. The rise from a coal miner to a interstate common carrier magnate, a trucking tycoon, had been made possible by Ashland's cunning and scores of eighteen-wheelers rolling freight across the pavement of the United States.

Ashland's personality and outward appearance was a lesson in deception. He looked more like a Baptist preacher than a ruthless businessman. His shiny white hair flowed back along the right side of his head in a wave that was seldom out of place. His sideburns were always cropped at the top of his ears. And his eyes, in them danced the magnetism that swayed many a competitor to sign a deal before he made full and conscious evaluation of it. He was a fast talker, quick lipped and shrewd, with a verbal delivery that almost made anyone he talked to look skyward for the impending onslaught of hellfire and damnation. But before the doom came, Dermont Ashland had secured that for which he had come. And that was the Ashland way . . . dazzle 'em and dominate 'em.

Ashland leaned forward in his chair and touched the intercom button that buzzed his secretary outside of his office.

"Yes, Mr. Ashland?" The woman's voice said.

"Shirley, is my limousine ready?"

"One moment, Mr. Ashland, and I'll check."

"Thank you." Ashland leaned back against the high-back leather chair and spun around slowly. He clasped his hands together and rested his chin on them, his elbows on the arms of the chair. He looked out the window across the Louisville skyline. There he saw the interstate highway with trucks and cars moving like ants working in and out of a busy hill. A smile parted his lips and he nodded his head. "Soon. Very soon."

The intercom buzzed on his desk and Shirley's voice came across the speaker. "Mr. Ashland, your driver is ready."

Ashland answered without turning around in the seat. He continued to focus on the skyline across the city. "Thank you, Shirley. I'll be out for the rest of the day. I'll call you when I get settled in."

"Yes, sir," Shirley replied. "Any special instructions before you leave?"

Ashland felt the smile on his lips widen. "Only one. If anyone calls for me, tell them I can't be reached until tomorrow at the earliest."

"Yes, sir. Have a good rest of the day, Mr. Ashland."

"Thank you, Shirley. That will be all."

Ashland studied the scenery for a long moment. Then he dropped his hands and stood from the highback chair. He walked to a private elevator ten feet from his desk. When he worked the digital combination, the door opened and he stepped inside for the ride to the underground parking garage beneath the Ashland Industries building. The door closed and the elevator started the smooth decent. When it stopped a minute later, the door opened into the private parking area. Ashland's driver, dressed in a chauffeur's uniform of dark coat, hat, and pants, stood expectantly beside the rear door of the black Lincoln Town Car limo.

"Where to this afternoon, Mr. Ashland?" The driver asked cheerfully.

"Churchill Downs, Howard. I have a meeting there in one hour," Ashland replied.

"Yes, sir, Mr. Ashland," Howard said. He opened the rear door and waited for the old man to get comfortably seated. Satisfied that he was, Howard closed the door and got in the driver's seat. The limo was already running and Howard slipped it into gear. "Gonna watch the ponies again this evenin', sir?" Howard asked.

"Yes, for a while. A mixture of business and pleasure. I always enjoy the horses." Ashland said as he flipped through a report folder he had carried from the office.

"Been a beautiful day for the races," Howard said in an effort to strike up conversation. "Not a cloud in the sky outside. Ponies ought to run quick."

"Yes, they should."

Howard inched the limo forward from the exit of the

parking garage onto the busy city street outside. He turned left and headed toward Broadway. Another left on Broadway and he saw the Third Street intersection in front of him. Howard made a left and headed south on Third. Several quiet minutes passed until Third intersected with Taylor Boulevard. Howard negotiated the right turn and drove along Taylor to the entrance of Churchill Downs. He drove beneath the giant sign that read: WELCOME TO CHURCHILL DOWNS— HOME OF THE KENTUCKY DERBY.

"Gate seven, like always, sir?" Howard asked.

"Uh, no, Howard. Not this time. Take me to gate three," Ashland replied.

"Yes, sir. Gate three is it." Howard drove through the isles of parked cars until he reached the entrance to gate three into the massive horse racing facility. He stopped beside the curb and jumped from the driver's seat. In a flash, he was beside Ashland's door and swinging it open. "I'll park, sir. Shall I join you or wait with the car?"

Ashland scooted to the doorway and stepped out. "Tell you what, Howard. I plan to be a while." He reached into the breast pocket of his suit and removed his wallet. He counted off several bills and handed them to Howard. "Here's a thousand dollars. Go have yourself some fun with the ponies. Meet me back at the car in three hours. How's that?"

"Yes, sir," Howard said. His eyes illuminated and he smiled as he accepted the money without question. "I'll be back here in exactly three hours. Thank you, sir."

"Very good," Ashland said. He smiled at Howard and walked toward the entrance to gate three.

Inside the sporting facility, Ashland made his way to the box seats and found the one he had reserved. He sat down, watched the ponies on the track, and he waited.

Ten minutes passed and a man came into the box arena. He moved through the isles until he found a seat two seats away from Ashland. The man was sinister-looking . . . dark complexed, dark hair, and very not-icable ghosts from teenage acne. He looked straight ahead at the track when he spoke to Dermont Ashland. "Good afternoon, Mr. Ashland."

Ashland also kept his eyes on the track. He spoke to the man without ever acknowledging his presence with his eyes. "Good afternoon, Ramone. What do you have for me?"

"Good news," Ramone said. His voice was cool, callous. His eyes stayed fixed on the track. "They are moving the microreactor even as we speak. I have men on them. We will have it in our possession by this time tomorrow. We will be in control of every vital compo-nent of the facility within twenty-four hours."

"And then?" Ashland asked.

"And then we will be in position to complete the project. Then we will be in control. Permanently."

"Good. Have a nice day," Ashland said.

"And you also, Mr. Ashland." Ramone stood and walked away. His eyes and Ashland's had not met through the entire conversation.

Two minutes passed and Ramone disappeared. An-other man came from the opposite direction and stopped behind Ashland. "Yes, sir?"

"Frank, did you get all of that?"

"Every word," Frank said.

"Good. When we have control of the facility tomor-row, kill him. He knows too much."

"Yes, sir. It's done," Frank replied, and he left the way he came.

———

The trip along the beltway in Washington had gone smoothly enough. But then that's the way Marc and Carl had planned it. They had waited to leave Washington, D.C., near midnight, both preferring to drive at night instead of in the daylight. And if their timing was right, they would arrive in Huntsville sometime in early afternoon.

Traffic on Interstate 66 westbound was the usual Washington madhouse until the Highway Warriors reached Interstate 81 near Strasburg, Virginia. Marc drove the Leeco Freight Lines customized overroad rig and Carl rode shotgun on the passenger's side. Interstate 81 had far less traffic than I-66 when Marc turned the rig south. Thinner traffic was welcomed, but the trip along I-81 brought back memories from a time at the beginning of their war against the scourge that ravaged mankind. Both men knew that further south, near Raphine and Steele's Tavern, if it were daylight they could look to the east beyond White's Truckstop and see the mountain where Carl almost lost his life in the first of their many challenging wars. That was a long, long time ago, and time had healed the wounds. The experience, however, was etched in their minds forever.

"You know something, bro," Carl said. "I was just thinking. Can you imagine what some of the terrorists we've encountered in our lifetime could do with a little device like that thing back there in the suitcase? Can you?"

"That's something I'd rather not think about," Marc replied. "The world has enough kooks in it. Give some of them with enough money a chance at something like that microreactor and the world would suddenly loose all elements of safety. There'd be nowhere to hide. Damn frightening, isn't it?"

"Yeah, that's an understatement," Carl agreed. "How we gonna work it when we get to Huntsville?" Switch shifts or both stay and alternate sleep scheds?"

"Doesn't really make any difference to me. You decide. I just know I'll rest much easier when I know that stainless steel timebomb is on its way into outer space. Babysitting instant disaster isn't exactly my idea of a good time."

"Look on the positive side, bro," Carl said. "Twelve

or thirteen hours from now that little gem will be safely inside the Marshall Space Flight Center in Huntsville."

"You say that like there's nothing to worry about," Marc said.

"Is there? You heard the general, nobody knows this thing is rolling. Right?"

The first shots ricochetted off the side of the rig before Marc could answer. He glanced into the mirror and cut the rig hard right onto the shoulder. "Wrong!" He yelled as he fought to control the speeding Leeco Freight Lines overroad rig.

"What the hell is that?" Carl yelled.

"Shooter coming up fast on the left. An eighteen-wheeler. I see two in the cab. Gunner on the passenger's side." Marc manhandled the steering wheel and kept the rig from crashing into the guardrail. He swerved back to the left and came back on the highway. He immediately implemented a zig-zag pattern back and forth across the highway. The rig screamed from the stress of sudden turns and shifted weight. The 1400-horsepower diesel power plant gulped diesel fuel and belched out high-performance torque in the process. Marc watched the road ahead and glanced every couple of seconds into the mirrors to keep track of the culprit.

"Rat shit!" Carl shouted. "Where'd he come from?"

"Beats me, but we gotta take him down before he causes one hell of a mess on the superslab. It may sound trite, but something tells me this is no chance encounter."

Marc steered hard, the Leeco rig groaning from the sudden strain. The other eighteen-wheeler crowded in close along the left side of the high-tech Leeco rig. The gunner in the passenger's window leaned out and fired an automatic weapon, his image visible in the peripheral light from the rig's headlights. Hostile bullets whizzed through the air and slammed harmlessly into the Armor-shield body coating on Marc and Carl's rig. The technically advanced body armor could repel the small arms fire as effectively as BBs off of an army tank.

"We could outrun him," Carl shouted.

"No. We mess up with forty tons of speeding overroad rig and we could kill a lot of innocent people. If we crash, the reactor could become unstable. Or at least I think it could. I don't really know that much about the thing. It's not worth the risk."

"Then I guess we shoot it out, huh?"

Action on Eighteen Wheels!

Marc Lee and Carl Browne, ex-Delta Force anti-terrorist commandos: They've taken on bloodthirsty Middle Eastern terrorists...deadly drug cartels...vicious bikers...the Mafia...no matter how badly they're outnumbered, Lee and Browne always come up swinging...and blasting!

Don't miss any of the exciting books in Bob Ham's OVERLOAD SERIES!